Planetary Devel

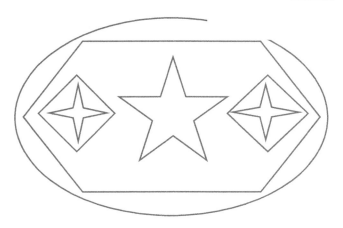

Asteroid Belt is Created

Vol 1

Ford G Strange

Jacket art by: Getcovers.com

This is a work of fiction. Names, characters, places, and incidents either are the product of the author's imagination or are used fictitiously, and any resemblance to actual persons, living or dead, business establishments, events, or locales is entirely coincidental.

ISBN: 979-8-9907842-9-1

eBook version available

Body text Baskerville

Published by
Planetary Developers Publishers LLC
Temple Texas USA

Perspective is an odd thing
   The one we're told
      The one we're taught
         The one society gives us
            The one we can see for ourselves

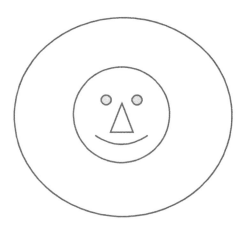

Table of Contents

PDV-041 The Kentz

PDV-041 The Kentz pulled into its final berth in the orbiting space port. The vessel would be decommissioned the following rotation after a brief ceremony and reception with the crew and former crewmen who served on her. Commander Nottap called out, *"Comms, clear all channels for an announcement."* *"Aye, Sir."*

After all the channels fell silent, a boatswain's whistle sounded from the PA system, *"Attention all hands, this is your Commander. I want to say thank you for your dedication to the Kentz. We are in port. Secure your stations and relax. The dining hall will be available until 17:00.*

A ceremony and reception will be held here tomorrow morning at zero eight hundred in the forward dining hall, dress in your class A uniform. After the ceremony and reception, bonuses will be awarded, and our status will be changed to off contract. Clear out your cabins of uniforms and personal belongings.

We're home, men, enjoy the rest of your rotation, and we'll see you at zero eight hundred, carry on." With that, the Comms operator switched off the PA system. Commander Nottap stood up and faced the bridge crew, *"Secure all stations. After that, you're dismissed."* They responded, *"Aye, Sir."*

Nottap entered his cabin, and his PDT vibrated. He looked at the message, *"Commander, you have been selected to Command the new PDV. I wanted to be the first to congratulate you. They are building a management group now. Congrats, Byron."*

He smiled, *"Yes! Now's my chance to show them all."* Looking in the mirror over the basin, he turned on the cold water, and rinsed his face.

He looked at his eyes in the mirror and thought, *"I hope he's not there when I walk in. "The baby of the family? That's how you encourage or validate me?*

Cupping his hands he rinsed his face and thought, *"It's mom's fault she refused to allow me to join the Neiubo Military. Oh, so now I'm "The Explorer," and you wonder why you get zero Father's Day cards. I hate coming back home."*

He stepped off the boarding ramp, walked to the shuttle dock, and check the schedule. The next shuttle to the surface would arrive in one hour. He thought, *"Layover lounge looks good."* As he walked in, a sign flashed, *"Open seating."* he sat at a table and looked at the posters and the news screen.

The posters depicted a space battle on an unknown gray planet with Galactic Military Troopers blasting a large caterpillar like insect that was attacking them, it had several rows of teeth and sharp claws. The caption read, *"VOTE YES! For the seventh branch of the Galactic military."*

He thought, *"Seventh Branch? Sounds like they're getting ready to take over more planets."* He watched the news feed, it showed a time lapse video of the new Planetary Developers vessel being built.

A host walked over and sat a glass of water down on the table, *"What can I get you, Commander?"* *"Good day, mate, I've been craving your double float burger and squares, thank you."* *"Aye, Sir, I'll get that and be right back."*

As he looked at the news feed, the narrator spoke of several vessels which had called for immediate assistance, they were being boarded. When help arrived, they found the crews lifeless bodies floating in space and the vessels gone. The Governance of Navigators Corporation assumed these vessels were boarded by privateers or another hostile group.

They had no information to indicate which but were attempting to locate the vessels. After trading barter tickets for his meal and shuttle ticket he stepped onto the shuttle. The overhead speakers reminded travelers of the inherent dangers of space travel, this made him chuckle.

On his way to his parent's house, he decided to stop at McCoy's for a shot or two. As he walked in the door, a woman had her back to him and he was smacked in the face with a back hand punch. He instinctively grabbed the hair on the back of the assailant's head and pulled her to the floor.

As he held his assailant down, he looked up, and a woman was charging toward him. He put up his hand to ward her off, but she ducked and slapped the head of his assailant. A man and a woman grabbed the charging woman pulling her back. His assailant jumped up and kicked at the woman.

Nottap and his assailant fell backward into a booth, she sat on his lap and began to squirm as she yelled at the other woman. The couple pulled the other woman to the back exit, and they fell out the door and into the alley. Nottaps assailant stopped squirming and sat on his lap. She said, *"Let me go, or buy me a drink."* Nottap grabbed the back of her pants and hoisted her off his lap.

She spun around and looked at him, *"Well, hello, sailor, when did you get in?"* *"Hello, Rhoda. I see you are keeping busy."* *"Aye Capitan, so wat ya drinkin these days, eh."* *"That's the worst accent I have ever heard. Are you still the bartender here or a barfly?"* *"Nope, to both. I own this place now."*

Nottap stood up, *"Well, congratulations on moving up in the world, good for you."*

"*Ha, hold that thought, the two best days of owning a bar, the day you buy it and the day you sell it double gin, right?*" "*Aye matey, arg.*" Rhoda laughed and walked behind the bar and poured the drink. He followed her and sat at the bar and, looked around. Rhoda said "*It gets packed at 18:35 and goes heavy until 23:45 exactly.*"

"*Oh, exactly wow how did you manage that?*" "*I guess you missed the new fabrication yard two blocks east. They end rotation at 18:00 and seats are full at 18:35 exactly.*" Nottap laughed, "*I'm glad you landed on your feet.*"

"*Ha, hold that thought, by the way I never properly thanked you for helping me with the court marshal. I know if it wasn't for you, I would have been in confinement for a long time.*" She walked around the bar, spun his seat around, and pulled him toward her. She gave him a hug and a kiss on the lips.

He hugged her back for a moment as she continued the kiss. He grabbed her by her upper arms, pushed her back gently, and stood up. "*Don't start your trouble. I still have the dang tattoo.*"

Rhoda smiled and said, "*You're getting soft Nottap, you kissed me back.*" "*I did not!*" "*You did too.*" "*Did not!*" "*Well, I'm going to tell people you did.*" He looked at her and realized she still knew how to push his buttons.

He laughed and said, "*We had good times together, I miss them, I miss you.*" She smiled, "*We did, I miss you too it's too bad things went sideways on us.*" He turned and looked at her reflection in the mirror that hung behind the bar, "*Yeah, Captain what's his name messed it up for us.*"

She turned and looked at his reflection in the mirror, "*He sure did.*" As they stood side by side looking in the mirror, at the reflection of each other they smiled.

She said *"Hey, what if ... ""Yeah, I better get to my ..." "Right, ... Your Parents house, you better ... ""I'll need my ... ""It's by the door... it's in the booth ..." "Yup ... there it is ..."*

He walked to the door and flung his duffle bag over his shoulder. Turning to look at her he said, *"Thanks for the drink." "Sure, stop by when you get back, we'll catch up, Oh, thanks for chasing off, ... Sorry about the punch..." "Sure, no problem. I'll see you when I get back. It's a short run ... be back soon."*

He threw her a half salute with a peace sign and she threw him one back. As he walked to the corner of the block he had a smile on his face. As he stood at the corner waiting for traffic to clear he noticed he felt ... *Happy.*

As he walked in the front door to his parent's house his mother greeted him with a kiss on the cheek. "*Oh, do I detect a little celebration libation on your breath?*" "*A little.*" She walked to the kitchen counter and rummaged in her purse. He put his duffle bag down by the stairs and sat on the couch.

She walked up behind him and handed him a mint, "*Thanks, Mom.*" She rubbed his shoulders and neck, "*What's her name?*" "*The Kentz.*" She swatted the top of his head, "*Not your ship, the woman who put lilac perfume on you.*" He laughed and said, "*Nothing gets by you. You're still as sharp as ever.*"

He reached back and held her hand, "*Is he here?*" "*HE, your father, yes, HE, is here, out back getting the grill ready. Listen son, you two have to bury the hatchet, both of you, for my sake.*" He let go of her hand and crossed his arms. "*Son, please, you're not going to be home long, so please, get along with your father.*"

"*For you, I will. Who is coming over?*" "*All of your brothers and their wives, it's going to be so good to have you all under my roof again.*" She walked to the kitchen counter and rummaged in her purse, "*By the way what ever happened to Jessabelle,*" "*MOM, her name is Kathy and she is, I don't know, somewhere in the fleet. I don't keep track of her.*"

She walked up behind him, leaned over and kissed his cheek, "*That's my boy, all grown up.*" "*Thanks, Mom.*" She slid an info card down his shoulder, "*Something to read when you have downtime on your new ship.*" He looked at it, *Match Makers Global*, "*Mom I can't ...*" she cut him off, as she walked to the kitchen.

"Son, you keep picking losers or boozers, I'm sure they are wonderful, well, females, check it out, and look outside the fleet. What is Jessabelle's rank Petty Officer?" *"Chief Petty Officer 1976."* *"Son, that's my point, not even a real officer, check it out, for me."* He imitated putting a blaster to his head and pulling the trigger. *"I saw that,"* she yelled from the kitchen."

Neiubo

Planetary Developers were humanoids that lived on the planet Neiubo, located in the Ophiuchus solar system, Milky Way Galaxy. An average planet, it measured forty-nine thousand miles, and the humanoid residents stood twenty-five feet tall. Neiubo had a planet wide industry.

The bulk of the residents of Neiubo worked to build large space vessels for population transport. Other residents provided services and goods for the workers. When a world was dying of natural causes or was facing impending danger due to a cataclysmic event.

Planetary Developers would offer a contract to transport the population or a portion of the population to another planet to colonize in exchange for raw materials. Their goal was to save as many lives as possible, and receive compensation for their service.

They would also search for areas of space in which a planet could be formed and used elements found on most planets suitable for humanoid habitation to start the formation of a planet.

Life on Neiubo was abundant, and like other planets of average size, there was room for all types of species. Their skills for building a planet were legendary throughout the galaxy.

PDV Crew Members

Planetary Developers Vessels crew members were generally residents of Neiubo, who were career-minded individuals with an adventuress spirit that applied to join the Planetary Navigators Corporation. Each applicant had to pass several entrance exams to test their physical fitness and mental acuteness.

If accepted, they would sign a twenty-five year *"Commitment to Serve"* contract and enter the Planetary Navigators Academy. Training mirrored the Neiubo Naval Academy standards and lasted four years. After graduation, postings to vessels and positions were assigned by the Governance of Navigators Corporation (Gov of Nav Corp), a branch of the planet wide Governance.

They managed space fairing guilds, vessels, and crew. Each cadet received training for three positions, which allowed them to be posted to any vessel in the fleet. Should they desire a more technical posting, they would submit an application, and if accepted, they would receive the specialized training upon returning to port from their current assignment.

Most PDV crews were off world for up to four years per voyage and aware of the inherent dangers of space travel. Both men and women were eligible for training in any position. Upward advancement of careers was always encouraged including command levels. PDV Command Officers were generally lax as they had worked with the same crew on previous vessels right out of the academy and were more managers than overseers.

Orientation

After the decommissioning ceremony on the Kentz, Commander Nottap rode a shuttle to the Planetary Developers Academy for vessel orientation. As he arrived and walked to the main doors, he noticed hundreds of other crewmen walking in and thought, *"Wonder what else they have going on."*

He scanned his ID card, and the gate opened. As he walked in, the info board showed *"PDV-109 Orientation"* with a flashing green arrow pointing to his left. As he continued down the main hallway with hundreds of crewmen, Academy Proctors blocked the walkway. A Proctor yelled, *"The lower levels are full head up to level four or five."*

As he reached the fourth level, Proctors said, *"Fill the first available seat, we are about to start."* He found a seat on the eighth row and sat next to a female crewman. The din of conversations was loud, and she asked, *"Do you know how many crewmen are on this Maiden Voyage?"*

He looked at her and said, *"No, I don't, I didn't get a crew profile with my contract." "Neither did I. This is listed as a limited crew for the Maiden Voyage, so how big is this new vessel?" "I don't know, maybe they're using a full crew for the Maiden Voyage. I know the normal compliment is two hundred, Command and Crew."*

A voice over the loudspeaker said, *"Welcome, crewmen, this is the Orientation for PDV-109, we will begin in five ticks. Proctors close the doors."* The din of conversations lowered.

A massive screen lowered from the ceiling. The image of an Admiral standing on stage appeared.

"I will answer your first question, two thousand five hundred. That is how many crewmen are assigned for this Maiden voyage." A loud murmur of voices swept through the auditorium.

"As you were, as you were, I will answer your second question: this state-of-the-art PDV is six thousand eight hundred miles in diameter.

PDV-109 is the largest transport vessel we have built. If successful there will be more." Murmured voices, now mixed with clapping filled the auditorium. As the sound of voices lowered, he said, *"It comes with all the bells and whistles everyone has been asking for and I am confident this vessel will be the first in a long line of titanic vessels."*

The crewmen murmured and applauded. The Admiral walked toward the right side of the stage and shook hands with an engineer wearing a teal green uniform. The Engineer walked to a podium on the left side of the stage and said, *"As you were, I am the Senior Engineer for this build. So now, "let's get technical."*

He pushed a button and the large screen showed PDV-109 in the space dock. *"We, have received hundreds of suggestions to design a more aggressive vessel, such as a bird of prey or a flying serpent. Those designs look fantastic, I agree, but they're not efficient. They require more engines and thrusters and have, on occasion, gravity voids or wells.*

This lack of gravity will cause the crewmen to become weightless and float around their compartment. We transport passengers, and having passengers weightless and floating around a section would not be good.

Once again, our vessel is a sphere for the following reasons. One, everything in space is round, including planets, stars, comets, and everything. Why, you ask? It takes less energy to traverse space. Two, everything in space rotates. If it rotates, it has poles.

If it has poles, it has a magnetic field in a torus shape, and if it has a magnetic field in a torus shape, it has gravity.

11

The third reason is energy flow lines, or lay lines. As the energy lines intersect, they grow a lattice. This process is organic. As the lattice grows, the charge or pulse of energy gathers strength and becomes measurable." He walked to the other side of the stage. An animation of PDV-109 in flight appeared on the screen.

"Our vessel spins, but the inner shell isn't connected to the outer shell. A layer of mercury separates the two shells. When it's spinning, it creates an energy lattice. Mercury is conductive and adds more plasma to the engine and other components. A little side benny, it also repels lead when energized.

Most privateer vessels have a lead-lined hull. The mercury will keep them from ramming our vessels as mercury repels lead. When the shell stops spinning, the lattice dissipates. When PDV-109 arrives at its destination, the shell will stop spinning and the flight crew will hold the orbit mechanically. The gravity will be artificial. Now let's talk power source."

After he explained the new engine types, he discussed the navigational shielding. Two hours later, he finished with a pictorial display showing the new crew quarters cabin layout, which received applause from the crewmen. A Proctor walked up behind him. The Senior Engineer saluted and walked off the stage. The Proctor said, *"Alright, we will break for lunch. It's 12:30 now. Be back and in a seat at 14:00. Dismissed."*

As Nottap stood up, the female crewman said, *"Let's get something to drink after we use the restrooms." "Okay, that sounds good. I can't believe the size of that thing, it's mind-boggling."*

She chuckled, *"That's putting it mildly. I'm glad we get a vanity and wider quarters with a data port and sonic shower. It's about phase." "I agree, it's about phase."* All PDVs were not military related and didn't transport Military Troops, equipment, or supplies.

A debate between Gov of Nav Corp and Neiubo Admiralty about the sphere design stalled as neither side had conclusive facts to support their position. The Admiralty wanted an aggressive design to ward off pirate attacks. The Gov of Nav Corp wanted a spherical shape for speed to outrun the pirates. They compromised, more deck gun batteries.

The massive biosphere could accommodate three and a half million twenty-five-foot residents for as long as forty years. When the transported population was measured under twenty-five feet, the interior could be changed to accommodate them, adding to the number of passengers that could be taken on board.

The PDVs had state-of-the-art deflective shielding that protected the vessel from space debris and defensive systems to block focused radiation beams. The auto-defensive systems would destroy rockets and projectiles fired by hostile forces and an armory of various weapons the crew could use to defend themselves should they be boarded.

Commander Nottap

Gov of Nav Corp selected Commander Nottap and his management group to oversee PDV-109. All the Kentz managers declined to serve under Commander Nottap again. They listed in their evaluation reports that his strict management style was more militaristic than they were accustomed to.

His failure to gain their loyalty was caused by his attempt to emulate his father, Neiubo Military Forces, SLS Brigadier General S.G. Nottap, a war hero with many decorations and honors. His mother refused to allow him to join the military, and she knew how to touch his heart.

Her husband and four sons were all the Neiubo Military Forces would get from her. At family gatherings, his brothers called him *"The Explorer,"* which sounded better than the baby of the family but still had a demeaning tone. With this new opportunity, Commander Nottap was determined to redefine his leadership style.

He aspired to be as bold as his brothers, and saw this role as the perfect platform to prove his mettle. He envisioned a more laissez faire approach, one that would inspire his team and earn their respect.

Growing up in the shadow of his father, as an army brat he learned how to travel light as the family moved from base to base every four years. His mother was determined to raise him in a traditional civilian lifestyle. This was always awkward for him and his brothers.

Making friends was a challenge as his schoolmates were army brats and finding common ground with them became harder as he grew older. His brothers decided to train him in the art of war out of the view of their mother. This brought the brothers closer together and he was able to adjust to his dual lifestyle.

As his oldest brother came of age and joined the army he struggled with the feeling of loss. The five brothers always knew the day would come when they each left the family home to start a new life, but dealing with a deep sense of loss put him in a state of depression.

He found comfort in the company of female classmates as they helped him develop and explore his feelings. His father and brothers became uncomfortable talking about feelings as most warriors only have two.

As a vulnerable schoolboy he also learned lessons of female manipulation which cost him his virginity at a young age, but having a dual lifestyle he knew how to keep a secret. When he was in the tenth year of his general education he noticed three older boys circle around a classmate.

As he watched they began to shove his classmate around, pushing him into each other and shoving him away. Nottap walked over and grabbed one of them by the arm and swung him around, *"Pick on someone your own size."* He reached in between them and pulled out his classmate. The largest of the older boys squared up to Nottap and asked, *"What are you going to do about it?"*

Nottap looked straight ahead, at the boy's throat and whispered, *"Make you bleed."* The boy stepped back and looked at him. The other two boys laughed. As the older boy turned to look at his friends Nottap struck him on the jaw and the boy dropped to the floor.
The other two boys stopped laughing and looked at their friend lying on the floor. They looked at Nottap and charged him simultaneously. He remembered hitting them both several times, but as he sat on the examination table in the nurse's office, clearing his head, he couldn't remember who won the fight.

He noticed his classmate sitting in a chair holding a bloody cloth under his nose and his head tilted back. He asked *"Did we win?"*

His classmate looked at him, stood up and walked over to the sink. He picked up a hand mirror from the counter, walked over, and held the mirror up to show him his face, *"No."*

Nottap took the hand mirror and started looking at his face, and said *"What happened to you?" "I stepped in after you knocked down the big one. We managed to take out one of the other two, but the others showed up ... there were to many of them. I'm glad those girls came to our rescue." "The Others?" "Yeah, their friends."*

"How did we end up here?" "Three girls carried you. One, help me walk here. Those all your girlfriends?" "Yes, but not at the same time, and not like that, at different times, well, except for, I meant, maybe the ... Nah, just friends now, same class, it's complicated."

"Oh, well, they seem very fond of you and thank you for stepping in and pulling me out." "You're welcome, it seemed like the right thing to do and I'm PSM427, my house name is Scott." "Nice to meet you, I'm PSM373, my house name is Byron. You gave us a bad boy rep now and they won't pick on us again. Especially after we bled all over them, made them look foolish."

He lowered the mirror and looked at him, and said, *"Right."* When his fourth brother joined the army and left home, he knew the sense of loss was nothing compared to a broken heart. The day after he graduated from general education, he applied to join the Planetary Navigators Corporation and was accepted to the Planetary Navigators Academy.

He ascended his career faster than his academy classmates and joked they should work for him, *"You should start calling me "Commander" now."*

The Tradition

It was a tradition on Neiubo a person could not to use their Family Birth Right Name to be appointed to leadership positions or higher career status. Each person had to earn their status through their skill or talent.

Only those who tested for entry and passed successfully gained entry to the Planetary Developers Academy. Promotions and rank also had to be earned. The tradition arose after a war based on families with the same last name as an original builder. Their family members received an appointed position as determined by the household elders.

Families that claimed leadership based solely on their Family Birth Right Name didn't necessarily have intelligent or talented offspring. The descendants were put into positions of power because they were born into privilege and had family wealth, they lacked the skill to govern fairly.

They began to corrupt all the levels of government, which caused many Neiuboians to become part of a class hierarchy and formed separatism. This oppressed many Neiuboians, and they rebelled after a corrupt politician was exposed for massive fraud.

They formed groups, and skilled laborers became skilled warriors and killed the oppressors, their minions, and private armies, the war was short.

The Short War

Prior to the short war, Commander Nottaps father, S.G. Nottap was a skilled Engineer Fabricator. He worked at the Lasko plant in Cosron for many years. When the war began it was a chaotic group of many factions, they all wanted change in leadership. He organized a group of his own, trained his followers, and attacked many estates.

Stories of his victories and leadership spread far and wide, more men and women joined his group. Some factions melded in with his group. As the ranks of his army swelled to match the size of the private armies of the elite his victories grew, along with the death toll.

He was known as *"Old blood and guts"* as he and his army gave no quarter and accepted no surrender from the private armies. After the short war a new form of governance developed. The people decided on a Council structure of representatives which would prevent one person or a select group of people holding all the power to make decisions for the masses.

They held office for five years, but could campaign for re-election if they were out of the council for five years, and had proved their talent as a decision maker. Residents that desired to campaign for a Council seat had to submit to a background check and have their qualifications verified, prior to campaigning. They had to show they were competent and not only popular.

Governance of Navigators Corporations was formed to manage affairs for space faring guilds on Neiubo.

This industry provided the bulk of the planet's wealth which was shared by those who contributed to the planet wide industry.

The people agreed this tradition would prevent any future wars and allow all Neiuboians to live in peace and have the same opportunities, family prosperity was determined by their skill level, labor or abilities. Gov of Nav Corp had a strict policy,

The Name Rule, it was put in place to adhere to, *"The Tradition."* This rule was the most violated rule which forced Gov of Nav Corp to hand out harsh punishments.

First Officer Crawford

PDV-045, The Rennat, was scheduled to be decommissioned upon returning to port. After completing their assignment, they set navigations to Neiubo. Commander Crawford sent a request for re-assignment to the first available vessel, however he didn't want a short run or low orbiting assignment.

Gov of Nav Corp offered Commander Crawford a contract to fill the position of First Officer aboard PDV-109 during the maiden voyage only. He accepted the post after reading the first two pages of his proposed contract. The other pages were standard procedures for the position of First Officer.

As this was a single voyage assignment and a temporary demotion, he felt it wasn't critical to review them. The turnaround would only be six hours, and PDV-109 was berthed in space dock CPP-109. He planned on staying in the *"Layover Lounge"* on the space port until it was time to launch, which appealed to him.

He knew he never wanted to live on Neiubo again after his three wives and six children were killed during the short war. Thirteen years ago, S.G. Nottap was referred to by his men as Major Nottap. They chased a private army into the small town of Yemdaca, where Crawford and his family lived.

The private army troops forced their way into private homes and used the homes as strongholds. The battles were fierce as Major Nottaps troops moved house to house to shoot it out with them. Crawford was off world on his second voyage, relocating the Caines people as their planet was expanding to the explosion point.

When he returned, he found his town destroyed. He learned at the conclusion of *The Battle at Yemdaca*, the private army was killed, with no survivors, along with many of the civilian populace.

Major Nottap was considered a hero for his bravery above the call of duty. He put himself and a group of elite warriors in harm's way to save the bulk of his army. The men decided to promote him to lieutenant colonel. S.G. Nottap had no formal military training, and former Army officers recognized his natural ability to use tactics and warfare.

They joined his group and told him the titles would help the army grow. Crawford didn't share in the admiration others had for S.G. Nottap as reports began to surface. Nottap and his group fired indiscriminately as a group of civilians ran past to safety. It was unclear which group killed the civilians.

He searched for his wives and children's graves and heard a mass grave marker stood in the former center of town with names on it. He searched the marker and found his wives names in the middle of the marker. At the base, he found his kid's names, and they were not together.

He imagined his kids were separated from his wives, and scattered through-out the town. As the imagery grew in his mind, he could see his girls screaming with terror in their eyes as their brothers fought for their lives. A deep pain came from his stomach as if he was being gutted. He let out a loud guttural scream of pain and fell to his knees.

Tears flowed down his face, and his screams grew louder. Several people ran to him but stopped short as they had seen this happen to others many times. Some experienced the same and knelt while waiting for the screams to subside. Others came out and did what they could.

They carried him to the local tavern, the server said, *"Put him in the corner and leave barter tickets in the pickle jar to help cover his tab."*

Residents had become all too painfully familiar with the scene as many residents or families seeking their loved ones experienced the same agony.

After drinking heavily for several days and nights in the town tavern, Constable Standish woke him up and sat with him. They discussed family lineage and legacy. Crawford told him about his three wives and six kids.

Constable Standish said, "*Either you are delusional, or that switchel is affecting your mind in the worst way.*" "*How did you end up with three wives and six kids?*" Crawford replied, "*They asked me to marry them at the same phase. Do the math for my kids.*"

Constable Standish laughed, "*Alrighty, I'll order an ambulance.*" "*Hold on there, Constable, I'm serious. Can I explain?*" Constable Standish sat back in his chair, "*Please do.*" Crawford ordered a fresh pot of tea with two cups. Standish sipped his tea, "*Go ahead, this should be entertaining.*"

Crawford sighed, "*When I was younger, I was in the dating scene looking for the right lady to marry. Well, I was dating two ladies, and I was honest that I was seeing someone else, that didn't bother them. While on a date with Karen, we ran into Dianne.*

It turns out they knew each other from the Higher Learning Campus and became close friends. Sister's close is the way they put it. They told another lady, Hannah, who was career-minded and seeking a part-phase husband. She had a career to follow and didn't have time for a full relationship. The three of them asked me to marry them, and without thought, I said Yes."

Constable Standish laughed, "*Yeah, I bet it was without thought. So let me ask you two questions: was your life full of frolic, and you smiled every day?*" Crawford gave him a deadpan look and said, "*Three wives, three honey, please do lists, no, not full of frolic, but I fell in love with them, what's your next question.*"

Standish stopped smiling and leaned toward him, tilted his head, and in a somber voice asked, *"How would your wives and kids feel if they saw you in this condition?"* Crawford's eyes went blank as he stared down at the table, he looked away and asked for the check. The server sat it on the table and walked away, as he reached for it, Constable Standish picked it up.

He looked at the check and called out to the server, *"Louellen, you put your private comms link on the check? seriously, woman?"* A female voice called back, *"He would clean up nicely, I'm positive of that."* Constable Standish sighed and shook his head. He walked Crawford to the door and held it open.

Crawford stepped out, and Standish said, *"Fair thee well, Sailor."* He walked across the street to the Travelers Center and reserved a shower. He stepped into the stall and cleaned up. After leaving the Travelers Center, he walked back into the tavern and tapped the server on her shoulder.

Louellen turned around, and he handed her a stack of barter tickets, *"Your tip."* Louellen blurted out, *"You're handsome, I knew it, I get off at 18:00 we can go to my place, and I'll freshin'"* He raised his hand and said, *"I'm busy."* As he walked up the street, he turned to look at the former town center monument.

He thought, *"I'm not a vengeful man, S.G. Nottap, but one day fate will give me what I'm owed, and I will take them from you as you took mine from me, this I vow as my heart is pure."* He shook his head and said, *"Never again, I am owed!"*

As he walked to the shuttle terminal, he noticed he felt hollow inside. As he looked at a little girl being towed by her mom, she smiled at him. He forced a smile back at her. As he watched them walk away, he noticed he felt ... *nothing.*

After getting a shuttle to the spaceport, he found a Planetary Developers support vessel in need of crewmen and signed on as an Engineering Tech. While they navigated to Alpha Ursa, Pirates attacked as they crossed the quadrant boundary. Crewmen manned the deck guns and sent out a barrage of plasma balls, which had no serious impact on the approaching vessel.

As their ship pulled alongside the support vessel, a blast came from the pirate's vessel and the cargo dock doors were blasted open. Pirates free floated into the cargo dock. Crawford gathered crewmen to accompany him to the cargo dock to engage the Pirates.

He stood behind several crates and watched as both sides fired wildly at each other. He thought, *"Is this happening? All this shooting, and nobody is getting shot?"* he grinned and watched until a shot splintered a crate above his head.

As both sides ran out of ammunition, a Pirate drew his blade and charged. Crawford shot the charging Pirate in the chest, he fell face first on the deck with a whump, sliding on his blood. A voice called out, *"That's not sporting, mate, your side is out of plasma, what say we settle this hand to hand, like honorable men, aye?"*

Crawford laughed out loud, *"Wait ... you have an honorable man in your crew?"* At that moment, a shot hit Crawford's blaster and knocked it out of his hand. The Pirate called out, *"Looks like we're square, mate. Here's your choice, jump into space or get carved up. Die whole or die in pieces."*

The Pirates charged across the dock, and the PDV crewman charged toward them. Crawford grabbed a chained jay hook and ran toward the Pirates. The fight was brutal and bloody, Pirates slashed throats and bellies, PDV Crewmen cracked skulls and smashed faces with the stock of their blasters.

Crawford strangled several Pirates with the jayhook chain and killed the last two Pirates by stabbing them with the jayhook.

He scanned, looking for more Pirates, and noticed everyone was down, and several men groaned. He looked out the dock door at the Pirate ship, and they flashed a light at him.

He was raising his hand to make an offensive gesture at them when thirty Pirates jumped from their ship and, free floated toward the cargo dock.

Crawford turned and ran toward the dead Pirates. He picked up as many blades as he could carry. He thought, *"Silent Assault."* After he gathered as many blades as he could handle, he turned off all the lights in the dock and disabled the control box. The emergency lights turned on, and he hid in the dark, waiting to attack, one by one.

After losing count of the Pirates he gutted, stabbed or slashed he had enough of killing and made his way to the dock control panel. He put on an emergency air tank and pushed the plunger, deactivating the atmosphere barrier.

All the bodies, blasters, unsecured crates, and several Pirates hiding in the dock, were sucked out into space. After activating the barrier, the atmosphere began to stabilize. He felt sharp pains on his legs and hands, looked down, and noticed he had cuts and slashes.

The roll up bay door opened, and PDV Crewmen and Medics entered the dock. They found Crawford at the control panel, and Medics treated his wounds. A Crew Chief told Crawford the Pirate ship turned and flew off after the debris blew out of the dock.

Medics stood looking at the bloody deck and walls, imagining how fierce the battle was to cause such a bloody mess. Gov of Nav Corp promoted Crawford to Commander for his bravery. He saved the lives of the Command staff and half the crew.

The promotion was honorary, as he didn't test or apply for the rank, but those who knew of his acts of bravery and how he used stealth tactics to kill the attackers drew the respect of many Commanders.

They signed a petition for an *"Exceptio regulae"* and submitted it to Planetary Navigators Academy for review. Academy Administrators and Promotion Board members reviewed a video and crew statements. They accepted the petition and declared the promotion valid.

On the voyage back to the Neiubo space dock, he spent most of his down time reading the Planetary Developers Personnel handbook. He felt the best way to repay the Commanders and Gov of Nav Corp was to be an honorable Commander worthy of their gift.

While his shipmates congratulated him and thanked him, he smiled in appreciation but noticed he felt ... *Nothing*. He wasn't happy, sad or prideful, he felt like, *"This is how it is now."*

His father sent him a video message, *"Hello Son, your Mum and I watched the newscast about the Pirate attack on your ship. We're happy you're alive and proud of you for defending your ship and crewmates.*

Here at home, they are calling you a Naval Hero and will be awarding you a Metal for Uncommon Bravery. A Young lady named "Louellen" left some gifts for you. I ate one, and it was tasty, see you when you come home." After thirteen years, he has yet to step foot on Neiubo.

PDV-109 Maiden Voyage

Their destination was the Chiappaletine nebula, their task, was to collect gasses, liquids, and metals. Their purpose, was to test the performance stress limits and load capacity. Normal operations for PDV vessels are population transport. The engineers designed this task to emulate a full load of passengers.

Most maiden voyages are mundane, to eliminate boredom, each vessel carries a minimum crew of two hundred, which gives each crew member several tasks and responsibilities. PDV-109 was no ordinary vessel.

The assigned crew of twenty-five hundred would be required to perform several tasks and monitor several stations and systems. A vessel this large could develop gravity wells or air leaks. The layer of mercury between the outer hull and inner shell could be a hazard if a leak occurred.

Engineering Department was responsible for the mechanical systems and power flow, it was also the largest department on the vessel. Engineering Manager Schmidt walked into his office and noticed a map of the engineering department on a touch screen. He touched the index and the screen listed ten thousand eight hundred monitor locations.

This made him step back and gasp, he thought "*Oh crap, I have a limited crew for all this? One Manager and crew for all this?*" He touched the scale index and the screen showed "*Sixty-eight-thousand-mile shell No Maintenance Needed. Eight control centers, coverage area eight hundred fifty-mile radius.*"

He muttered, "*Oh, that's right, Maiden Voyage with a limited crew, note to self, one manager, one control center. We're empty, no passengers.*" He relaxed and check the maintenance schedule.

It showed the location of drive carts and a map. The map looked like a race track. He stood up, laughed and said, *"Fun City."* Launcher Section was the smallest department on the vessel and considered a section and not a department for that reason. Yeldarb, the Section Manager, walked into his office and opened the schematic file for the launcher.

The launcher, a high energy tube that could expand to any length with a broad orifice opening for loading. As he read the file a smile grew. He realized this was the largest launcher he had seen and imagined firing it from one planet to another. He read the last paragraph and, reality set in.

He muttered *"There's always a catch, maximum launch power requires two point four million terahertz of plasma with the shell at full rotation. Well, that's not happening."* After closing the file, he opened his PDT to review the launcher crewmen assigned to the Maiden Voyage. The file showed all the assigned launcher crewmen were former Troopers, he thought, *"Not one FNG, excellent."* He chuckled, put his feet on his desk and leaned back in his chair.

Planetary Scientists on board were specialists in various fields. Science Manager Gazou entered the Science Department. He looked at the state-of-the-art computers and logged in. As he looked at the department layout, he couldn't help from saying *"Wow, this is awesome,"* each time he opened a new file.

After reading his mission goal and guidelines he let out a laugh. He stood up and stepped back from the control panel. He looked at the department as he stepped in a circle and called out, *"My wildest dreams have come true,"* with a wide smile on his face.

Projectile Specialists were explosives handlers and demolition Engineers. Projectile Specialist Manager Newsome opened the overhead roll up door and walked in. The first thing he noticed was the shine and gleam of all the new equipment.

He squinted his eyes and looked for the backwall. He looked at the floor map for this section and noticed the location for his office. *"It's going to take me ten ticks to get there if I walk. This thing is massive."* he muttered.

After looking at the floor map he noticed a location for drive carts which was next to the main entrance. He walked a short distance, and found rows and rows of new drive carts. They all shined as they were recently built. After finding a drive cart labeled *Manager* he got in, pushed the button on the destination panel for *Managers Office* and the ride began.

The task for this department is to assemble parts sent by Engineering Fabricators using a schematic sent by the science department. The projectiles could be used for gas collection, liquid collection or disperse elements in an area of space to cause a chain reaction. Impact projectiles were stock inventory, no build required.

Fabrication Engineers, a branch of engineering, would build parts from a schematic sent by the Science Department. After the fabricators built the parts, they would bring them to the Projectile Specialists. The Specialists would assemble the projectile and take it to the Launcher section.

Call for Assistance

On the bridge, Communications Officer Porter, in his eleventh year of his commitment to serve contract, returned from shore leave to his new assignment as Communications Officer aboard PDV-109 for the maiden voyage only. As he was setting up his profile on the communications panel, he intercepted a transmission.

It was a conversation in progress, and it sounded urgent. He turned and looked at Crawford and said, "*First Officer, Sir, you might want to hear this.*" Crawford, stood up from his command chair and walked over to the communications panel. "*What do you have?*" he asked. "*Not sure, Sir, but it sounds like a planet is being invaded, and it's in a solar system we will be passing through.*"

He connected to the comms panel and they listened to what appeared to be a planet requesting immediate assistance with an unknown hostile race. Unable to determine what either side was referring to, Crawford notified Nottap.

"*Commander, Comms picked up part of a communication which may be a planet under attack or, is being invaded, we might want to alter course around that solar system.*" Nottap connected to the comms panel and listened as a representative for planet Aden described their need for military assistance to a Galactic outpost officer.

He turned on the intercom, a direct line to the Launcher Control section. "*Launcher Control, do you copy?*" "*Aye, Sir, Launcher Control here,*" responded Launcher Tech Dodson. "*Aye, this is the bridge, launch a probe to Aden to view the planet surface, Comms will send you the coordinates, and send the connection information to First Officers PDT.*"

Dodson, the Launcher Control Tech, acknowledged with a crisp "*Aye, Sir*", and a click was heard when he turned off the intercom. Nottap looked at Tracker and said, "*Nav, maintain course toward the nebula, slow our velocity to one quarter and we will be launching a probe.*"

Navigation Officer Tracker replied with a firm "*Aye Sir.*" Tracker had used his PDT to upload his profile into the navigation panel. His assignment to PDV-109 was his fourth voyage. His career plan for the remainder of his service was to accept short trips.

After Dodson launched the probe, Tracker followed it on his navigation scope. The probe pierced a water membrane that surrounded Aden with no problem. Planet Aden was the fifth planet of the Copernican solar system that orbited a solar star (sun).

Crawford searched the Neiubo database and found a file on Aden. He looked at Nottap and said, "*Sir, I have information on Aden.*" Nottap replied, "*Aye, display it on the forward screen.*" "*Aye, Sir.*" As they watched the information, it was displayed in a documentary format. Nottap looked at Crawford with a quizzical look. Crawford replied, "*Aye, Sir, that's all I could find.*"

Mysteries of the Universe

With your host Leonard

Hidden Gems of the Copernican Solar System

The Copernican solar system is comprised of: The Solar star Zeus, Mercury, Venus, Minertha, Mars, Aden, Jupiter, Saturn, Uranus, and Neptune.

This solar system has an inner and outer solar system. Mercury, Venus, Minertha, Mars and Aden are considered the inner solar system. Jupiter, Saturn, Uranus and Neptune are considered the outer solar system.

The outer solar system planets are average size planets measuring between forty-nine and fifty-two thousand miles in measured diameter.

Mercury, the first planet from Zeus, has a measured surface diameter of three thousand miles and is the iron core of a planet. The planet was pulled into the solar stars' gravity zone and the intense heat burned off the mantel. Planetologists determined Venus, Minertha, Mars and Aden will experience the same fate.

Venus, the second planet, has a measured surface diameter of three thousand eight hundred miles and is covered with lava. Planetologists confirmed the mantel is being burned off.

Minertha, the third planet, has a measured diameter of eight thousand miles and a water membrane around the planet. This gives a visual appearance of an ocean world. The membrane prevents long range scans, bouncing the signals into space.

Aquarius Oceanographers sending Heavy or large profile probes to the water planet discovered the water membrane turns to ice when touched, deflecting or destroying the probes.

Mars, the fourth planet, also has a measured diameter of eight thousand miles and a water membrane.

The membrane provides the occupants of these planets with an abundance of fruit and vegetables, which is good as the adult male and female humanoids stand forty-feet-tall.

The water membrane is a living entity much like fungi, and from the ground looking up resembles an ocean. Mars conducts trade with several planets in the Taurus system exclusively and are a very secretive society denying requests from Planetologists and, Oceanographers to study the planet and water membrane.

Aden, mirrors Minertha in physical attributes and societal customs. They have more of an open trade policy but, restrict visitors to historic sites and monuments areas only.

These three planets are hyperbolic chambers and Planetologists can only estimate the population at four million per planet. They theorize these planets are rich which gems, diamonds and quality ore as the hyperbolic chambers cause pressures used by mineralogists to refine raw cut gem stones.

Mineralogists have nicknamed these planets, "The hidden gems of the Copernican solar system." Thank you for watching Mysteries of the Universe with your host, Leonard..."

Crawford chuckled and said, *"Sir, their planet is only eight thousand miles in diameter. They are forty feet tall, how do they all fit?"* Nottap said, *"Thank you, First Officer, return the screen to Navigation mode." "Aye, Sir."*

Premature Launch

Tracker turned to face Nottap, "*Sir, we can go around the entire solar system, however, that will add two cycles to our voyage, both coming and going.*" "*Negative Nav, maintain our course.*" "*Aye, Sir.*"

Crawford said, "*Sir, there are some obvious questions about this situation, but rerouting would be our best option.*" "*Aye, perhaps First Officer, but is that our only option? We should explore the possibility of answering their call for assistance. We are Neiuboians, and helping is what we do.*"

"*Aye, Sir, we do help when we can, but this situation involves a hostile race attacking another race, and we can't be a planet's defenders.*" Nottap looked at Tracker and said, "*Nav, can we pass through the solar system while maintaining distance from this planet?*" "*No, Sir, the navigational charts for this system have not been updated.*"

Tracker looked at more navigational charts and said, "*Sir, the information First Officer displayed shows the Copernican solar system, with small planets between Jupiter and the solar star, but our charts show six moons around Jupiter, and Jupiter is the first planet from the solar star.*"

Crawford replied, "*Aye, Nav, let me look at this posting. This information was posted by a Greek two hundred cycles ago, when was our chart last updated?*"

Tracker pulled up the navigation chart for the solar system, "*Sir, a Greek posted this chart nine hundred cycles ago before the planet-wide storm raged on Jupiter,*" Tracker looked at Porter and said, "*Comms, can you make contact with Jupiter?*" Porter replied, "*Negative Nav, the clouds are ionized and my signal is bouncing back.*"

Crawford stood up and walked to the navigation panel and sat in the second seat. He scrolled through the nautical charts and attempted to find the shortest reroute.

Tracker looked at Crawford and said, "*Sir, the nearest slip tube is five thousand miles away, but we must turn around now and return to it.*" "*No Nav, no backtracking.*" "*Aye, Sir.*"

Crawford swiveled his chair to face Nottap, "*Sir, let's break this down, one, the Aden planet is eight thousand miles in diameter, which equals twelve thousand eight hundred kilometers, and the Aden people stand Forty feet tall. I would like to see how they all fit on a planet the size of a grain of sand, but if they can't handle the invasive species with a stature of forty feet and we stand at twenty-five feet, what could we do?*

Two, we don't have the crews assigned to take passengers and where would we take them? Sir, I suggest when we arrive at their solar system, we go "Silent Ops" and keep going." Nottap stood up and asked, "*And the probe we launched? What do we do with that?*" "*Aye, Sir, that may have been premature, but we ignore it and keep going.*"

"*Aye, First Officer, that may have been premature, but it's out there, and I won't ignore it. We won't refuse their call for help, we will refer them to others who can help. Nav maintain our course.*" "*Aye, Sir.*"

Nottap walked over to the comms panel and said, "*Comms, ignore any hails from them for now.*" "*Aye, Sir, and you received a message. I sent it to your PDT.*" Crawford and Nottap returned to their command chairs.

Nottap leaned toward Crawford and said, "*This is quite the pickle we're in.*" Crawford looked at him and smiled, "*Aye, Sir.*" Crawford leaned toward Nottap and whispered, "*What do you call a fuzzybella with no legs?*" Nottap rubbed his palms together and looked at Crawford, "*I don't know, what?*"

"It doesn't matter, he won't come when you call him." Nottap groaned and whispered, *"I hope that's not your best, yikes."* Crawford said through a chuckle, *"Nope, that's my warm up. I have a bar joke, you'll like this one. Four guys are walking down a street, three guys walk into a bar, and the fourth one ducked."* He looked at Crawford, *"I don't get it."* Crawford chuckled, *"You will when you least expect it. One more."*

As he whispered to Nottap, Pilot Logan and Copilot Windstorm looked over their shoulders at them. Nottap blurted out a muffled laugh, *"Now that's funny."* Copilot Windstorm looked at Logan and gave a thumbs up, Logan smiled and winked at Windstorm, *"It's always a good sign when the command staff get along."*

Crawford stood up and walked to the Engineering panel. He opened the schematics file for the PDV and scrolled the screen. He made notes on his PDT and downloaded a map he found in the *"Visitors Brochure"* file.

Nottap walked up behind Crawford and leaned over his shoulder, *"What are you planning First Officer?"* Crawford jerked and looked to his left at Nottap. *"Apology, First Officer, I didn't mean to make you jump, what are you planning?"* he asked.

"Sir, I am marking a route to perform a walkthrough, we should know our vessel and department locations, care to join me?" *"Aye, let' do that."* Nottap called out, *"Pilot, maintain course and you have the bridge."* *"Aye, Sir."*

Crawford and Nottap entered the lift, as the doors closed Windstorm set his panel to auto pilot. He looked at Logan, *"Why do they always put you in charge when they leave the bridge? Commander of PDV-088 did the same thing, every time."*

Logan looked at Windstorm and made a haughty sniff, "*I have a corona of maturity and Command presents about me, that's why.*" "*Oh, because your old and Granddads have great wisdom?*" "*Okay, I'll take that, Aye, that's why.*" They both laughed.

Pilots Logan and Windstorm

As a senior Pilot, Logan was nearing the end of his commitment to serve contract. After completing his last voyage on PDV-088, he was at the plaza relaxing. His PDT vibrated, when he received a request for flight deck personnel. He opened the message and selected PDV-109.

After reading the description, he sent his profile to Gov of Nav Corp for consideration. He had included in the special requirements section, "*Sirs, I would like to bring with me Copilot 7005. He is available for hire, and we are on the top ten Pilot-Copilot list, Thank you.*"

The Gov of Nav Corp accepted Logan's profile and sent him a service contract with a note attached. "*Your request is Granted. Inform C.P. 7005 to submit his profile with Reference Code CCP-109.*"

Logan had served in the Neiubo Military as a young man and rose through the ranks. He was decorated with many medals for bravery as he received wounds in two battles fighting the Morton's. After recovering, he went back to the front line. After reaching the rank of Captain, he turned down a promotion to Major.

He didn't want a desk job, he preferred to be near the front line with his Troopers. After his wife of many years died from contaminated water and food, he no longer has a zest for the military. Many people assumed the elite class had devised ways to kill the populace by putting Florida in the water and sea coral in processed food as a preservative.

After her funeral, he resigned as a Captain, a week after he resigned, the short war began. He had enough of battle and stayed out of the short war. The day after S.G. Nottap declared victory over the elites, he applied for and was accepted to the Planetary Developers Academy and began his new career.

He sent a message to his friend Windstorm, whom he considered a son he never had, to send his profile to the Gov of Nav Corp for the position of Copilot. He noted, "*In the special requirements section, insert this message, See Reference Code CCP-109.*"

Logan noticed on the posting this assignment would only be for the maiden voyage. Upon returning to port, the appointed commander could extend the posting. There were no crew profiles attached to his contract.

Windstorm was at the park with friends and neighbors for a cookout when his teenage daughter Sara handed him his PDT. He noticed Logan's message and opened it. After reading the message, he asked his daughter if she would mind if he accepted the post.

The posting was set for two years, meaning she would live with her grandparents while he was away. She agreed to the posting, as did Windstorm's parents. During the short war, he and his wife joined Liberty for All. The group stormed an estate belonging to a notorious and corrupt politician.

A sniper killed his wife Becky, as they entered the courtyard. He raised his daughter with the help of his parents, Sara was two years old at that time. After the short war, he applied for the Planetary Developers Academy and was accepted.

He served on several PDV support vessels as an Engineering Technician until he was selected to attend flight training. His trainers considered him a natural and sent recommendations, the Training Staff posted him as a Copilot.

Logan and Windstorm met during a flight competition. Logan was the overall winner, and Windstorm placed a close second. At the end of the competition, Windstorm was in the canteen when Logan walked over and sat at his table.

He introduced himself, and they began to talk. Logan ordered meat pie and switchel for both of them, Windstorm never had either. They hit it off and became close friends.

Windstorm's career as a Copilot had a rocky beginning, his last two Commanders made notations. Windstorm was an excellent Copilot but took too many chances when assigned to pilot the vessel. As the Copilot he would need to fly the vessel while the Pilot used the forward blasters as defensive weapons.

His Commanders always felt confident with his flying but grew concerned he would take one hair-raising chance too many and crash the PDV. That was until he met Logan and flew as Logan's Copilot. Logan calmed him down, and the two became one of the top ten Flight Deck teams.

As a team they won top tier races, making them the favored team on the betting board. Their only loss was to team Granger, a father-daughter duo that held the Neiubo World Cup for flying.

Sorry, who is this?

Asecond call went out from Aden to all the planets within the solar system and the Galactic Council, Porter began to record the message. The Galactic Council Receptionist, Laura, answered the call, her voice eloquent and beautiful, "*Salutations, Galactic Council how may I direct your call?*"

A hesitant male voice said, *"Yes, we need help."* She responded with an apologetic soft voice, *"Sorry, who is this?"* The male voice, shaky and broken said, "*Robert ... from Aden.*" Laura sighed and said in an annoyed voice, "*Salutations, Robert from Aden, how may I direct your call?*"

The male voice cracked as he said, "*Yes, this is Robert from planet Aden, but you can call me Rob. We need help.*"
She hesitated in her response and said, "*Excuse me but, help in what manner?*" The male voice now sheepish and quiet said, "*An unknown race is attacking us.*"

Laura sighed and said in a low eloquent and beautiful voice, "*I see you're calling from an unregistered planetoid, and your request will take some phase to explain. I will transfer you to the general help desk. Stand by, and gratitude for calling the Galactic Council.*" Laura put Rob on hold, and he listened to celestial harp music.

"*General help desk, Olivia speaking, what is your crisis?*" said a female voice in a matter-of-fact tone with sounds of power tools in the back ground. "*Salutations, this is Rob, from planet Aden. An unknown hostile force is attacking us. We want help to defend ourselves, please hurry,*" his voice now confident and casual.

"*Well, Rob, sorry that is happening to you and your people. I see you are calling from an unregistered planetoid. I need more information about your planet, such as your navigation location and GNC number.*

41

Let's start by registering your planetoid to get your GNC number, I will transfer you to the Welcome Center, and Rob, gratitude for calling the Galactic Council." Olivia put Rob on hold, and he listened to celestial harp music.

A female voice said in a happy rhythmic tone, *"Salutations, welcome Center, Jessica speaking. How may I assist you?"* Rob replied in a casual voice, *"Salutations, Jessica, I'm Rob, from planet Aden. Our planet needs immediate assistance to defend against an unknown hostile force."*

"Oh Rob, I'm so sorry that is happening on your planet. Let's get your planet registered and issue you a GNC number. Oh, and Rob, it's our policy to investigate all new registrants prior to sending out our elite warriors." "Okay, Jessica, I understand. Let's do this, and remember this is an Emergency." "Yes Rob, they all are. What's your solar system Navigation Number or name."

After Jessica registered planet Aden, she sent a request for information to the Greeks who had observed this quadrant of the galaxy. Rob was transferred back to the general help desk.

"General help desk, Olivia speaking, what is your crisis?" "Yes, Olivia, this is Rob from Planet Aden. I have my GNC number now." "Salutations Rob, good to hear from you, go ahead with your number." "Okay, it's COP88st14.5 did you get that?"

"I did ... now we ...Oh, darn, okay, Rob, I see we have no useful information on your planet, and I know this is an emergency, life threatening situation for you and your people.

We will bypass the normal census data sheet, and I will send you to your Galactic Council Members' office. Stay on the line." "Okay, Olivia, and thank you."

Olivia called Galactic Council Member Synder's office. *"Salutations, Office of GCM Synder, Junior Aide Kerry speaking"* said a male voice with an air of superiority.

Olivia said in her midwestern voice, with a hint of annoyance, *"Yeah Kerry, this is Olivia from the General Help desk. I have Rob from Planet Aden on the line, his planet is in dire need of assistance from an unknown hostile force, help him out. Okay Rob, good luck and gratitude for calling the Galactic Council."*

Rob heard several clicks as Olivia disconnected from the call. *"Rob, is it?"* said the male voice with an aristocratic voice. *"Yes, from planet Aden." "Rob, not to be insensitive, but how close are you and your people to being extinguished?" "Um ... Well ... that's kinda hard to say, Keery, as we know nothing about them."*

"It's Kerry, I see, so Rob, are you sure they exist and this isn't some sort of ill-mannered citizen committing murders?" Rob was silent and stunned by the question. The haughty male voice said, *"Hmm, yes well, Rob from Aden, send proof of your claim to the office of Galactic Council Member Synder, and I will take a look at it before sending it forward, gratitude for calling the Galactic Council."* Rob heard several clicks as Kerry closed the comms link.

G.R.E.K.

Greks, also known as Greeks, are the keepers of historical records and are a timeless race of higher vibrational beings. They have held the role of historians for as long as they have existed. They live on many planets and are known by different names pretty much everywhere. Greeks are normally formless and take whatever form necessary to observe and record history.

Greek is an acronym: G.R.E.K., Galactic Record of Events Keeper. They witness history, write down the event in a book, which is given to the *Higher source of all things, the Creator,* and held in the Hall of Eternal Past. Greeks would also give a copy of the book to the historians of the planet on which the event occurred. Those historians, on almost all planets, had many Liber Haus or bibliotheca, which translates to Libraries.

The first Grek who replied sent a message to the Galactic Council: "*Aden is a small planet rich with resources, animals, other creatures, and humanoid life forms that do not appear to be much of a threat. The Occupants live under a water membrane that prevents long-range sensor scanning.*"

Upon receiving the messages from the Greks about the planet Aden, the Galactic Council, a governing body overseeing interstellar affairs, ordered a First Contact Summit for the Planet Aden. After assigning several Representatives for a proper First Contact group to address the people of Aden they ordered a Planetary Watch Vehicle to proceed to Aden for reconnaissance.

The Watchers

Planetary Watch Vehicles (PWV), are flown by trained observers known as *'The Watchers.'* The vehicles are equipped with advanced technology and can sustain the crew for a two-hundred-year mission. The Watchers are not your typical scientific observation group.

These augmented humanoids with wings had the unique ability to withstand the harsh mental riggers of prolonged space missions. They were primarily used for scientific study of a planet or, if recruited for military purposes, reconnaissance prior to landing on a *'hostile'* planet. Their uniforms had reflective composite material woven into the fabric, making them invisible.

Once they had located a secluded area in or around a city or military base, they would land, exit the vessel, and fly for several miles in different directions to observe and make notes. Generally, they didn't carry weapons, heavy loads, or other humanoids.

After arriving at Aden, the Watchers reported to the Galactic Council they found Grigorians on Aden, but no structures, such as hives, nests or tunnel mounds, that would indicate they had been residents of the planet for an extended period of years.

Long before the concept of *'time'*, the Army of Watchers discovered simple life, intelligent life, and life that showed potential to be intelligent on many planets. As this life began to jump from one planet to another, tracking their movements became cumbersome.

A Greek named Archimedes, well known as a tinker, thinker, and craftsman, invented a device that is still in use, the Trace Markers Sensor Scope. He and his father, Phidias, mass produced the TMS devices without the permission of the Higher Source, distributing them to all the Watchers. This device detected the base DNA, the first four DNA strands.

The Higher Source kept the DNA base codes within the Bibliotheca of the Hall of Eternal Past and only accessible to Watchers. A Watcher would enter the DNA code into the TMS device to find the location of a person or group of life forms.

The Watchers orbiting Aden used their TMS devices and found over half a million Grigorians on Aden. They reported to the Galactic Council and Greeks that the Grigorians were invading Aden, and many lower life forms also occupied the planet. Neither the humanoids nor the lower life forms would be corrupted by the presence of the GMF fleet or Troopers if the Galactic Council sent them to Aden.

A Watcher named Dnomyar, was watching Aden field workers when two disappeared. He turned on his TMS, and traces of Grigorian DNA flashed on the screen. Dnomyar noticed four children were walking towards the area and flew to them. He made himself visible to the children, telling them to turn around and run away. The oldest child said he was looking for his father and uncle. Dnomyar yelled at the child, "*Run for your life!*" The children turned and ran away.

Many Aden people began to notice humanoids that wore uniforms not from Aden and other humanoids that had wings and could appear and disappear in an instant.

Civil Service and Territory Representatives received several calls from the residents in a remote area about "*Strangers.*" Civil Service, the governmental body on planet Aden, sent a local Good Neighbor Safety team, similar to Police Officers, to the area to "*Have a look around.*"

The First Encounter

The Good Neighbor Safety team interviewed several people who claimed they had noticed strangers in the area. They discovered two groups of humanoids. One group was augmented, and the other was non-augmented. Rather than approaching the groups, they chose to contact the Military Base Commander in the area for assistance.

The Military Base Commander sent a small unit to make contact and investigate the activity of the "*Strangers.*" The unit leader, Sgt. Frazier looked over the remote area as Lance Corporal Luck drove the goinmover, "*Watch the terrain Corporal, all we need is six troopers getting sick in the cabin area.*"

"*Yes, Sir, that last pothole jumped in front of us.*" They both laughed. Sgt. Frazier pointed at an object resembling a giant golf ball perched on a tee. "*What's that over there? Stop here, and we'll approach on foot.*" Sgt. Frazier stepped out and walked to the rear of the goinmover. As the Troopers exited the deployment hatch, he had them follow him to the other side of the road and up a hill. All the Troopers used their telescopic lenses and looked at the object.

The speculation began: it was a new type of water tower, it was a new type of weather radar tower, it was a new type of energy transfer tower, it was a large push pin that you find on a map marking the spot, "*You are here.*" Sgt. Frazier laughed and asked, "*Who came up with that last one?*" the Troopers called out in unison, "*Burr.*" "*Alright, Pvt. Burr, take point. Luck and Perry, you have our six, as always. Burr, lead us to the, You Are Here push pin.*"

As Pvt. Burr led the group into the field, Pvt. Carlson said, "*Don't worry, Burr, I have your back.*" "*I thought you said don't worry, your shooting scores suck.*" The Troopers laughed as they walked into the field.

Corporal Luck followed Pvt. Perry, as Perry was the weak link in the squad. Sgt. Frazier assigned Luck as his *"babysitter"* during this assignment.

Corporal Luck pushed Pvt. Perry, *"Com'mon Perry, hurry up, again falling behind, why do you do this every time, Com'mon get going." "Don't push, I'm doing my best, why are you always in a hurry to rush into danger?" "It's what we signed up for. Keep going, talk and walk, talk and walk." "Well, I didn't sign up for that, I signed up to learn how to cook, I want to ..." "Yeah, I know you want to open a restaurant."*

As Perry and Luck fell further behind, Luck said, *"Ok, Perry, it's phase to pick up the pace."* A booming voice came from the sky in front of them, *"STOP! Turn around, behind you."* They both stopped, Perry stood close to Luck, *"Perry, get off me, you're too close, spread out."*

Watcher Dnomyar made himself visible to them, *"Turn around, look behind you."* He vanished in an instant.

Corporal Luck spun around and noticed two humanoid figures approaching them. They wore explorer group uniforms, but they had alligator heads. Luck pointed his blaster at one of them and yelled, *"Stop, hands up now!"* Pvt. Perry screamed, threw his blaster down, and ran towards the road. Perry ran faster as the sounds of blaster fire and screams filled the air. The sounds grew louder as all the Troopers engaged the Grigorians.

After reaching the goinmover he huddled behind the passenger side. He tried to open the door, but it was locked. A moment later, he heard silence and began to cry, in his mind, he knew the others were dead.

Trembling with fear, he began to jerk the door handle, tears in his eyes blurred his vision, and he wiped them away. He franticly scanned the ground for a rock.

The sound of a body skidding on gravel came from the road, Corporal Luck slid out from under the goinmover and Perry screamed in fear.

Luck pushed him away from the door and struck the window with the butt of his blaster, and it shattered. He grabbed the radio handset, "*We're under attack! Send...*" The transmission ended with a crackle.

As Aden Elite Troopers in armored vehicles arrived in the last known location of the small unit in the remote area, two survivors were spotted as they hid in a ditch. After medical treatment for injuries, Lt. Bronc took both troopers to the base commander, and both troopers told the base C.O., "*Alligator men attacked us.*"

The Investigator

The C.O. had them taken to the hospital for additional evaluation. A seasoned Investigator, well versed in handling such cases, was assigned to the case and went to the hospital to interview the two Troopers.

The Investigator walked into the hospital and was greeted by Lt. Bronc, "*Sir, we have the men separated for now and I take it you have read their statements?*"

"*Yes, I read them, alligator men, right?*" "*Yes Sir, shocking incident, if it's true.*" The Investigator asked, "*Lt. Bronc did the hospital personnel check their system for drugs or alcohol?*" "*Yes Sir, that was the second step after the examination for injuries. The results came back Negative for both Troopers.*"

"*Good, we can rule that out and was a psych test performed on both Troopers?*" "*Yes Sir, both passed, considering their mental stress from the encounter.*" "*Good, they're not delusional. Let me ask you, Lt. Bronc, do you know these men? I mean, have you served with them directly?*" "*No Sir, but their Platoon Leader and Lieutenant are now in the room with them.*" "*Good, let's start with Pvt. Perry, and if you don't mind, can you stay with me during the interviews as a witness?*" "*Yes, Sir.*"

The Investigator and Lt. Bronc walked into the room with Pvt. Perry. Lt. Bronc asked the Platoon Leader to wait in the hall. The Investigator asked Pvt. Perry to describe the alligator men who attacked them, focusing on one in particular. Pvt. Perry sipped water, cleared his throat and sat up in his bed.

"Well, Sir, he was my height, forty foot one, his head was a short snout alligator, his eyes were yellow with pupils that were vertical and black, his skin was, well scaly like a lizard and not an alligator, he had hands the same as ours with long nails, like blades, or spikes.

At a distance he appeared to be wearing a service uniform, like a mechanic or ground crew uniform but as he got closer, I could see his skin had turned to that and he wasn't wearing anything. You believe me right Sir? you do, right, Sir? it was real Sir."

The Investigator smiled, *"Yes, Pvt. Perry, I do, how did you get away from this man."*

Pvt. Perry made a hard swallow and cleared his throat, *"Well, Sir, that part is kinda fuzzy. I remember waving down the passing Trooper Transport." "Ok, Pvt. Perry, I'll have the Doctors release you when they have finished treating you. Rest for now."*

Lt. Bronc and the Investigator stepped into the hall. Lt. Bronc dismissed the Platoon Leader, sending him back to the base. He asked the Investigator what he made of Pvt. Perry's statement. The Investigator sighed and said, *"They're here on Aden, the Reptilians. The Intelligence Department has been looking for these beings, now we know what we are dealing with. I will contact your C.O. and file a report with him. I am recommending that Pvt. Perry and Corporal Luck receive an honorable medical discharge. They will receive full benefits of service due them, and I will ignore their acts of Cowardice unless they dispute their discharge."*

The Investigator looked at his tablet and made notes, *"Keep them here until their discharge papers arrive. We don't want them to talk with other Troopers about this as it will spread like wildfire, and the other Troopers will become Jumpy."*

Lt. Bronc straightened his stance, *"What acts of cowardice?"* The Investigator noticed Lt. Bronc had puffed his chest.

He didn't make eye contact and said, "*They ran, both of them they ran, kinda Fuzzy how I got away, how I survived, and the others didn't. It's an all too familiar theme, the brave parish while the cowards survive to tell "A Glorious Tale of the Soul Survivor."*"

Lt. Bronc glared at the Investigator, "*Cowardice is a serious claim to put on a Trooper. What proof do you have that they ran?*" The Investigator took a deep breath and sighed. He looked at Lt. Bronc and said, "*Well, Lt. Bronc, a Soul Survivor who didn't run, is the last man standing on the battlefield. They have a gaze with soulless eyes, and most must be dragged off the battlefield. It's if they are bound to the battlefield by blood or another mystical bond.*"

He stepped toward Lt. Bronc and said, "*Most importantly, they never tell "A Glorious Tale of the Soul Survivor." They do the opposite, they don't speak at all. You have to pull it out of them.*"

Lt. Bronc chuckled and relaxed, "*You think they saw the Bogeyman? They tell misbehaving children about this Bogeyman, and you're saying they're real?*" The Investigator looked at Lt. Bronc, "*Yes, they're real, look at the Troopers in the morgue, yes, they're real.*"

After leaving the hospital the Investigator went to the remote town. He interviewed the residents who made calls about the *Strangers* and the children who claimed to have seen an angel. The children gave a different account, each had a story that didn't match the other.

The Investigator wrote that off as child hysteria as the only similarity the children had was the statement, "*An Angel appeared to us.*" He submitted his report to the C.O. and the C.O. issued the discharge papers and forwarded the report to Civil Service. Civil Service sent a synopsized report to Robert, Director of the United Territories. Rob convened a gathering of the territories representatives after which he began to call for help from the Galaxy.

Galactic Council Member Synder

T he Galactic Council considered who occupied the planet first and also what kind of problem was this. A planet problem, a solar system problem, or a galactic problem. Aden was a small planet, a "*grain of sand*," unknown due to the water membrane. It had been overlooked or went unnoticed by vessels traveling through the solar system for eons.

Council members needed more information about Aden and recommended several calls be made to their neighbors in the solar system. They wanted to know are these planets the moons of Jupiter or are they indeed independent sovereign planets with no parental planet for protection or guidance.

They considered trapping the Grigorians on the planet rather than killing half a million or more highly intelligent beings. Once trapped, they could negotiate with the Grigorians on behalf of the Aden people. Galactic Council Member Synder received notice this planet fell within the boundaries of her cosmic responsibility.

GCM Synder had her aide Churchill gather information on Aden. He made several calls to known planets in the Copernican solar system. Jupiter was unable to answer as the planet was experiencing a planet wide storm. Neptune answered Churchill's call but didn't have any more information than what was already known.

Saturn responded to Churchill's request for information and sent a general report they were breakaway moons that orbited Jupiter. They were unaware if the moons had humanoid life on them, but surmised if they did have humanoids, they would stand one thousand feet high, which is normal height for Jupiterians.

They suggested Churchill should contact Jupiter directly for verification. After reading the report Churchill muttered in a sarcastic tone, *"What a splendid idea, why didn't I think of that ... oh wait ... I did ... glad you keep an eye on your neighbors' safety."*

Churchill called Rob, *"Salutations, Rob, I am Churchill, the aide for GCM Synder. This office has received a message that you and your people need military assistance. Is this correct?"*

Rob replied, *"Yes, that's correct. Are they on their way now?"* Churchill chuckled and said, *"No, my dear man, we need more information, such as how long you and your people have been on planet Aden, and what has your military planned for combating this "Unknown Hostile Force," and, most importantly, why have your Heads of the Planet waited so long to register with the Galactic Council? You see, Rob, the Galactic Council will not "Jump To" at your first call. What if this is a ruse, and you and yours think you have found a way to dispose of an enemy? Our Elite Troopers carry the most modern weaponry, and we won't send them in guns a blazin' on your say so. Am I clear? Do we have an understanding?"*

" Yes, Churchill, I understand, I understand we could be wiped out by the phase your Elite Troopers get here. Let me be upfront, will you help us or not?"

"Maybe, after we, the Galactic Council, determine if your claims to the planet are valid. Look at this from our point of view, Rob, we never knew your planet was there. So, is this your planet? We don't know, what if you and yours are the hostile force? Again, we don't know."

Rob sighed, *"Look at this from our point of view, Churchill. We know we can't defend ourselves from these "beings" or whatever they are, and we will all die unless we get help from a higher source or power who can defeat these "beings."*

So, tell me, Churchill, if you found yourself in this situation, how long would you be willing to wait?" "My dear man, this has nothing to do with me, this has to do with you and yours. I assure you if we, the Galactic Council, find your claims valid our Elite Troopers will rain on them like hell fire. I will contact you with our findings, and Rob, thank you for calling the Galactic Council."

After Churchill disconnected the call, Rob had a tight feeling in his gut. He looked at a picture of his family on his desk, and tears formed in his eyes. Rob pounded his desk with his fist, stood up and yelled *"We don't need you. You bureaucrats need us. We will find a way or make a way. We always do."*

Unintended Consequences

On the PDV, Crawford received a video message from his father. He looked around and noticed the others were busy. He opened the message, *"Hello, Son, your Mum and I are planning your welcome home party. I got your estimated return date from a friend who works at the Tracking Office.*

Before we get too far into planning, I wanted to know if you are at the end of your self-imposed sentence. It's been long enough, Son. Your Mum is the one you're hurting, not SLS Brigadier General. It's time to forgive yourself. You were being a provider for your family and you can't be everywhere at once.

I'm your dad and I have a good idea what you were thinking. You were thinking if you were home when the elite army came into town you could have saved your family. No, Son, you would be dead too. I know you would have killed many of them before they killed you, but no, son, they still would have been killed.

Look at this event from a different perspective. You are alive to carry on their memory. Every eve of the event SLS Brigadier General comes to town for a three-rotation ceremony. On the last day, a celebration is held. They celebrate the living who carry on the memories of those who passed. We miss you son, see you soon. Send a message when you can."

The message ended and Crawford closed his PDT. He scrolled the Engineering screen studying the PDV defensive systems. He thought, *"Unintended Consequences, self-imposed sentence. It's not a sentence. It's a vow, dang it, Dad. Now I'm thinking, yeah, why did I think this way? Well, at the time, I was hurting bad. Who am I hurting? Who am I hurting? You're right, Dad, dang it. I guess, well, me and Mum. I know they wouldn't want me to live like this.*

I have to keep my vow, or do I? Dang it, Dad, you always make me look at myself. Now that I think about my vow, that's the reason I never went back home. What if, what if I saw the General or his family, I would have to kill them. That's why I never went back, I know I couldn't go through with it."

He looked around the bridge and noticed everyone was looking at their monitors and thought, *"To thine self be true. The truth is, out here, among the stars and planets, I'm fulfilling my vow by waiting for an opportunity. I will limit my vow. If I see the General, I will kill him. I will find a way to get close to him, and I will kill him."*

Crawford picked up his PDT and recorded a video message. *"Hello Dad, I'll be coming home on that date, and I'm excited to see you and Mum. Things have changed, and ... so have I ... See you soon."* As he pushed the send icon, he felt ... *Free.*

Pocket Change

Porter called out, *"First Officer, Galactic Council Reps are requesting any vessel to transport them to the Ari estates solar system, ARIES constellation. They have resources for passage."* *"Aye, Comms, are they close or on our way?"* *"Negative, Sir, slight detour."* Crawford looked at Porter and said, *"Comms, that tells me nothing send it to Navigation, I want exact numbers."* *"Aye Sir."*

Tracker called out, *"First Officer, it would delay us by four rotations, picking up, transporting and dropping off."* *"Aye Nav, stand by for sub course."* *"Comms, accept their offer and send them an estimated phase of arrival."* *"Aye, Sir."*

"Nav, set a sub course to their location." *"Aye Sir."* *"Comms, who are we picking up?"* *"Two GCRs named Jank and Trop, they are augmented Sir."* Crawford sighed and said, *"Comms, I'm not a Dentist, why are you making me pull information out of you?"*

"Sir, my apology, GCR Jank is a faun, and Trop is a Centaur. They are requesting transport from the edge of the Taurus constellation to the edge of the Aries constellation to meet a shuttle, Sir." *"Outstanding Comms, now we're on the same page, well done."* *"Aye, Sir."*

Tracker called out, *"Sir, eta to pick up is two phases. Our travel time to drop off point will be two rotations, and two rotations back to this spot to resume our assignment course for a total of four rotations."* *"Aye Nav."*

Crawford looked at Porter, *"Comms, did you notice no dentistry required."* *"Aye, Sir."* He walked over and settled into his command chair, leaning in towards Nottap, *"Sir, how would you like to divvy up our pocket change?"* Nottap looked at Crawford, *"Well, First Officer, I'm not sure, I haven't dabbled in this "side job" business before."*

"Sir? You? A seasoned traveler, you've never taken a "Little Side Job? well Sir, I'm flabbergasted. I suppose this is the cycle you lose your virginity." They both shared a hearty laugh. Logan and Windstorm glanced back, Logan grinned and shook his head, Windstorm chuckled.

Crawford said, *"In honor of your first, you take sixty and I'll take forty. How does that sound?" "What? My virginity is only worth sixty percent?" "Well, Sir, you did wait until you made "rank."* They all shared a hearty laugh.

Galactic Council Reps

GCM Synder appointed Representatives from the Ambassadors Corp, a small group of political pollywogs with a desire to help, to gather on Neptune. She assigned them the "*First Contact*" task with the Aden leadership. The group began to discuss a "*Best approach method*" for first contact.

As they all studied different philosophies, they determined the whole group would go to Aden and meet with the Aden Leadership. Galactic Council established that Aden was a space fairing planet, however, whether they had encountered or had any contact with augmented humanoids was unknown.

The Galactic Council Representatives (GCR) group were from planets near the Copernican solar system. Not all planets sent a GCR, as they had little or no interest in a tiny planet the size of a grain of sand. Larger planets inquired if Aden was a moon and not a planet.

The GCRs were both augmented humanoids with various adaptations and non-augmented humanoids. Churchill sent several copies of the documents to the GCR group. Among the documents was a small hand drawn picture of a little girl holding hands with her father and mother standing in front of their house.

The little girl's name was Tami. "*We love our planet, save us*" was written across the bottom. The GCRs began to discuss the conflict on Aden, what the two races wanted, what role the GMF Troopers would play, and how the conflict could be resolved.

Karol, a non-augmented female, lived on Lilii Borea, an average-sized planet within the Ari estates solar system, ARIES constellation. She was appointed Chairman of the GCR group by GCM Synder and would report directly to Churchill.

During a group face-to-face communication, Karol asked Jank if he would be her assistant. Jank, a Faun, half man half goat with horns from the planet Epsilon, an average sized planet within the Tauri Union solar system, Taurus constellation, accepted the position.

Karol read a synopsized report to the group outlining the situation on Aden. After reading the report, she said, *"First contact with Aden came in the form of a standard voice comms, from a male Aden named Robert or Rob to the Galactic Council requesting help. This is a new planet, you can look up COP88st14.5 on your PDTs. It's more like a planetoid rather than a planet.*

Well, more like a moon, as it is eight thousand miles in diameter. Grigorians are now on the planet, and they are attacking humanoids. This is an emergency situation, so we must act quickly.

As you all know, the Grigorians are a planet clearing race of beings first discovered by Bud many cycles ago. I say we send a GMF Fleet and have them pick us up at Saturn. From there, we transport with them to Aden, and we discuss all matters on the Command vessel. What say all of you?"

Trop, a Centaur, half man half horse, from planet Aldebaran, an average size planet within the Tauri Union solar system, Taurus constellation, asked, *"I agree we need to move on this, but what is a Giggy ... gord ... orian?"*

Karol replied, *"They're called Grigorians, and they are augmented humanoids or insects that can look humanoid. Scientists haven't classified them yet."*

Jank said, *"I don't think they're humanoid at all. I heard they are reptiles with unique abilities to emulate other beings or creatures and are called Reptilians, or so I heard, I don't know for sure."*

Trop replied, *"How can we resolve this if we don't know who or what we're dealing with? We need more information on both parties."* Jank replied, *"I agree, let me pull up the information on the Grigorians."*

Several other GCRs from planets within the Milky Way galaxy, further away from the universe's hub, had never heard of *"Grigorians or Reptilians."* They needed more information to determine if the conflict was cultural, ideological, resource plundering, domination expansion, or biological.

In the Milky Way galaxy race has nothing to do with your skin color or your geographical location on a planet. Your base DNA determines your race. What you are made of, such as carbon base, crystalline base, iron base, copper base or zinc base. On most planets in this galaxy, the humanoid form is the dominant form.

The humanoid forms are non-augmented and augmented. Non-augmented humanoid form is one head, two arms, two legs. Augmented humanoid form is one or two heads, or other species adaptation head such as bull, ram, horse, monkey, fish, bird or dog. The arms and legs vary from four to six arms and legs.

All humanoids fluctuated in height, as height is determined by the gravity of the planet, oxygen level, and type of radiation the solar star in their solar system emits. On average, planets in the Milky Way galaxy have humanoids that stand twenty-five feet tall and are not better than other creatures that live on the planet.

They are more intelligent than the other creatures that live on the planet, which increases their survivability. In the Bud galaxy, reptilians are the dominant race. They are the superior predators on the planet and which ensures their dominance of the planet.

Jank said, *"The information regarding the Reptilians is extensive. Would you like me to synopsize it or send the complete file to your PDTs?"* Karol said, *"Jank, hold on that. Download it to a file, and we'll review it on our way to Aden. Alright, let's arrange a ride to Aden."*

Karol filled out an official request form for Galactic Military Intervention. She added that the GMF Fleet and Troopers needed to be non-augmented for safety reasons. She signed the order and sent it to GMF Command.

The order landed on the desk of Lt. Col. Vanwyke, he read the order and chuckled. Vanwyke called Lt. Col. Nelson and asked her to come to his office. Nelson leaned in the doorway and tapped on the door, *"Sir, you wanted to see me?"* *"Aye, Charlie, have a seat."* He handed her the order, *"You're gonna' love this."*

After reading the order, she laughed out loud and blurted out, *"Who's messing with you?"* *"I know, I thought the same thing until I received the sit rep."* He handed her a tablet, and she began to scroll the screen. *"Who sent you this?"* She asked.

Vanwyke laughed and said, *"A GCR assigned by Churchill. I guess he is still sore about losing his pants to me at the poker tourney. I told him that he shouldn't bet what he couldn't afford to lose."*

Nelson sat back in her chair, *"So, he didn't know your poker name is "Mr. Cleaners" I take it?" "He does now."* They both laughed. *"Anyway, Charlie, would you assign that to the Academy? They're always looking for a good training assignment." "Sure thing. Can I send a response to the GCR?" "Ha, that's why I thought of you. Have fun."*

Lt. Col. Nelson sent a reply, *"Galactic Military Forces Command, Lt. Col. Nelson, to GCR Karol, your order is denied. GMF Command can only receive orders from an actual Council Member. GMF Troopers are not separated or segregated by augmentation, and GMF Command cannot be mandated to do so.*

Planet Aden measured eight thousand miles in diameter and could not accommodate an entire task force in orbit. GMF Command will send our elite combat Expeditionary Force group to planet Aden. If the GCR finds this agreeable, resubmit an official request for Galactic Military Intervention.

For future reference, to avoid embarrassment, you should consult your Junior Diplomat Corp protocol manual before submitting Any Request to GMF Command." After reading the message, Karol hissed and said, *"That's rather pointy."*

The Battle for Aden

Lt. Col. Nelson began to organize units and vessels to be sent to Aden, Mars, and Minertha. The standard Task Force Fleet consists of one hundred fifty vessels. The three planets were only eight thousand miles in diameter.

All battle vessels were five hundred miles long and three hundred miles wide, and the crew stood twenty-five feet tall, both augmented and non-augmented humanoids. Each battle vessel had a working crew of five thousand Troopers, eleven thousand ground deployment Troopers, and two hundred fifty air attack vessels.

For normal sized planets, the battle vessels were appropriate in dimension. The overwhelming numbers of Troopers and firepower secured many victories for GMF Command. The GMF Army was a Volunteer Army of many different types of humanoids, augmented and non-augmented, men and women, from many planets in the Milky Way galaxy.

Volunteers signed an eight year or sixteen-year commitment to serve contract. They spent two years in basic training before they advanced to combat units. The training was for both body and mind, which gave them the upper hand on many foes who violated the Galactic Rule of Peace.

They served as combat Troopers for six years, after which the command would promote them to other non-combat units or specialized combat units or release them from service. The Rule of Peace prevented the spread of any one form of ideology by force.

Many millions of years ago, a group called the Morton's, led by a Pleiadian named Moroni, invaded a planet within their solar system. After killing the planet's leadership and demoralizing the armed forces command, they forced the people to accept their ideology or die. Once they had established rule over the people on the planet, they expanded their influence until it covered every planet in that solar system.

Wanting more, Moroni had his Morton's jump to neighboring solar systems. Morton's appeared to be friendly upon first contact with the occupants of a planet and were allowed to bring fellow Morton's to join them. When they had a sufficient number of missionaries, they attacked the leadership of the planet and forced the people to accept their ideology or die.

During the final battle between GMF Troopers and the Morton's, Moroni escaped by dressing as a woman and carrying two small children to a safety zone, boarded a vessel, and departed. Moroni is an immortal being who desires to be worshipped and idolized. The Galactic Council is aware of his childish endeavors, but he has not committed any crimes. He has his followers commit the crimes, which is why he is not pursued.

Lt. Col. Nelson had more significant issues to deal with and determined the only group to send was an Expeditionary Force. This force preferred the name Expedi Forces, and assigning them this task would be a problem. She called Major Whitman, Commander of the Training Academy, to her office.

Major Whitman tapped on the door, and Nelson looked up. *"Come in, have a seat."* *"Aye, Sir,"* She looked at Whitman, *"Galactic Council was notified by Rob, a Representative for the planet Aden, of an invasion in progress on their small planet.*

Aden is in the Copernican solar system, and the hostile force is described as alligator men, which may turn into a bug infestation.

Who knows why this became a GM problem. Use this as a training mod for recruits ready to graduate." She swiped her tablet, and Whitman's tablet vibrated. He looked down at his tablet and chuckled. He looked at Nelson, *" Well, that's different, but why use an Expedi Force?" "I'm curious." "You're curious, Sir?" "Aye, I want to know if the Troopers right out of the Academy can handle themselves."*

Whitman sat up in his chair. *"Well, Sir, I can assure you we are training them with the best tactical information and conducting tactical exercises on a regular basis. We also follow the GC rules of engagement. The Academy also monitors Troopers for one cycle after graduation."*

"Prove it. Use this as a training model. I want the next graduation class to fill the role of ground Troopers, and the latest batch of new Commanders will lead them." Whitman noticed she was covering a grin. He gave her a side glance, *"Charlie, you're bluffing, that's not why at all, your poker face is showing."* They both laughed.

She said, *" You're right, but I had you for a moment." "Aye, Sir, you did Sir, so spill it. What is the real reason." " My boss gave it to me to give to you. I am guessing Vanwyke wants me to get points for the next round of promotions. So, list this as a training mod, and we can both get points. He said you were always looking for a good training mod, and this should fill your request."*

"Oh, I see, that's why, is not because if he ordered a real Expedi Force, they would tell him to put this up his ..." She cut him off, *"Aye, that too."* They both laughed.

She said, *"The planet they will be going to is only eight thousand miles in diameter and an Expedi Force is the smallest unit we have."* *"Aye, Sir."*

She sat back in her chair and said, *"Also, keep this new group away from the real Expedi Forces, keep this information limited to the academy staff. We both know what would happen."*

Whitman chuckled, *"Aye, Sir, but it might make for an entertaining brawl."* They both laughed. Whitman assigned the newly promoted commanders to fill leadership roles, he also sent a note to Fleet Management and requested they assign older vessels for this training model.

Whitman addressed the newly promoted commanders: *"Gentlemen, this should be a short in and out operation. A planet that small, you should make quick work of it. Keep in mind, Senior Command will watch you as they are "curious." That's all I can say about that. Carry on." "Aye, Sir."*

Expeditionary Force units consisted of Troopers with at least seven years of combat experience. They were always the first in and the last out, this made them battle hardened and jaded toward regular mundane assignments.

The EF Commanders were always vocal with GMF Command when assigned a mission regular Troopers could handle. EF Commanders always wore a green beret, Lieutenants and Petty Officers wore a red beret, and Troopers wore a black beret to show Esprit de Corp for their Specialized Combat Unit.

The Expedi Force sent to Aden were issued a powder blue beret to show a temporary Combat Unit Status. Fleet Management told Major Whitman, *"Sir, the vessels available for your mission are one Command vessel, four trooper transport vessels, and one air support vessel with twelve air attack craft."*

Whitman replied, *"Aye, we'll use them."* GMF Engineering Corp sent three support vessels with Engineering troops with seven years of combat engineering experience for base construction.

Operation Suevas

Aboard the Expedi Force Command vessel (EFCV), all newly promoted command officers waited for their orders. They had gathered in the Command Conference room to relax and discuss their plans for furthering their careers. The officers checked the roster to determine which newly appointed command officer had the highest seniority and would lead this group.

They also would know where they fell in line in the overall command structure for this assignment. An excited, newly promoted Officer walked into the room. "*They arrived, our orders, sending them to your PDT.*" The Senior Commander, Lemmor, stood up and walked to the front of the room. He looked at the men and said, "*Make this easy on me. Change your seating based on our seniority.*

The most senior sits here." He pointed at the first open seat to his right. The Commanders shuffled about but knew exactly where to sit. "*Alright, let's take a look at this.*" He scrolled his PDT, and after a moment, he looked at the Commanders. "*Looks basic. The three highest senior commanders will stay with me on the command vessel. Everyone else will be assigned a base. Name it following GMF standards.*

This is our first mission, and the higher-ups will be watching us. Help each other out, and use private comms to request help from me or from each other. Remember, this is the first phase GMF has ever organized a group like ours, so let's not screw it up. I know you guys are the best at what you do, or you wouldn't be here.

The role of the Aden, Mars, and Minertha Military Troopers will be to support us with routine patrol and observation. Remember, the local military on these planets lack GMF training, and we will need to have patience when dealing with them. We know nothing about the people on these planets.

We only knew they were here once they called the Galactic Council. So, with that being the case, limit contact with them, and don't allow them near your headquarters or other sensitive areas. They stand Forty to fifty feet tall, let's make sure nobody gets stepped on, keep your people close to the base. Let's get to it."

Recovered Technology

Many years ago, on a planet ravaged by the Morton's, GMF Troopers stumbled upon a crash site and meticulously picked through the wreckage. They discovered technology that was utterly alien to them.

After Engineers painstakingly dismantled a device using reverse engineering, they finally unraveled its purpose. It was a location device that used DNA to find a person or a group of people or creatures that shared base DNA strands. Engineers tested the device by using the DNA of a missing person to find them, or their remains.

After one hundred successful recoveries of the missing, the device was certified and used to find victims of natural disasters. GMF Command wanted a rigorous field test and using a shadow market sold the devices to Bounty Hunters and Private Investigators. Both groups work without restriction of judicial procedure and skirt the line of official conduct.

The Private Investigators searching for a victim of a violent crime often found their remains. After securing the DNA of the perpetrator left behind on the victim's remains, they entered the DNA and tracked them down. When they found them, the Private Investigators captured them and brought them to justice. In extreme cases, after killing the perpetrator in a shoot-out, they would notify the authorities and request a body pick up.

Bounty Hunters, more often than not, had to chase down the wanted which always ended in a brawl. The device would fall or experience rough handling, and this tested the durability of the construction. Both groups were monitored for their success rate. Satisfied with the results, they issued the devices to the elite combat forces. GMF Command was largely in the dark about the Grigorian army's strength or technologies.

Most planets that had requested help had been devastated and conquered. Only a few planets had successfully repelled the Grigorians from their planet. Only in the aftermath of a victory was data collected. GMF Troopers had captured several Grigorians who had been wounded and drew DNA from them.

The DNA link that gave the reptilian shape-shifting ability remained a mystery to cellular biologists, but they did manage to uncover the base links. Armed with their own version of the TMS device, GMF Troopers were ready to face the Grigorians.

GMF Troopers loaded the base DNA numbers into their TMS devices, and embarked on a hunt for the elusive Grigorians. However, the Grigorians were not easy prey. Vessel engineers expanded on the hand-held version and equipped vessels with TMS devices.

With a wider scan radius, Grigorians could be found within a million miles. Grigorians were discovered on planets many portal jumps away but still within the Milky Way galaxy. GMF Troopers assigned the task of hunting the Grigorians were given one mission objective: Eliminate as many Grigorians as possible.

The initial stages of the hunt were grueling, with the Grigorians' space faring technologies and shape-shifting abilities posing significant challenges. Grigorians would shape shift into a humanoid form, which confused the Troopers, who were expecting to see a reptile or reptilian form.

As the Grigorian numbers depleted, they jumped from one planet to another, fleeing to many different planets. The Galactic Council was informed that the Grigorian population numbers had dropped, but resources used to combat them remained consistent. GMF Command had moved troops and resources to other conflicts, claiming the redeployments were related to the hunt.

Galactic Council was set to cut the funding in half, but GMF Command argued they had developed a seventh branch of the military during the hunt for Grigorians and needed the funding.

GMF Command posed to the Galactic Council that the reptilians were humanoids and followed the same strategy as the Mortons. A group of Galactic Council members stated they were cosmic bugs, and all funding and resources should stop, and this problem should be turned over to bug exterminators.

Galactic Council members brought in scientists with the assignment to classify the Grigorians as cosmic bugs or invasive insects. Using the known DNA sample, the Scientists couldn't determine the original origin of the Reptilians but determined they didn't have enough Humanoid DNA to be classified as human.

Council members argued that conflicts should be handled by bug exterminators, not military troopers or equipment. GMF Command brought in their scientists to verify the Galactic Councils findings. Their scientists' findings contradicted that of the Council scientists, and determined the Reptilians that ate a humanoid now had enough DNA to be considered human.

They could learn to negotiate or compromise. The Grigorians could also develop more human traits and emotions. GMF Command argued Grigorians are sub-human, with homicidal behavior that couldn't be corrected with traditional methods and only through evolution could they become more peaceful. Until then they must be hunted down and killed.

Galactic Council was embroiled in a heated debate over the Grigorians' population and their true threat to the Milky Way Galaxy. Questions plagued GMF Command: How did the Grigorians move so swiftly, evading capture or avoiding ambushes? What kind of weaponry were they employing? The most important question was, what was their battle strategy?

The aftermath data left Military Command with a crucial question: *'Was this an intelligent race or a cosmic bug?'* The willingness to negotiate differentiates an invasion of an intelligent race from a cosmic bug infestation. Like all military plans, the command had forces and equipment assigned and strategies for all conditions.

Every detail was planned for the warriors and weapons, which were ready, and the total eradication of the bugs looked assured. The Grigorians looked for planets to meet their needs, for concealment, and for food. Aden was such a planet.

Vessel Bound

The Galactic Council had issued orders to GMF Command to attempt negotiations prior to open warfare wherever the Grigorians were discovered. Aboard the EFCV, the GCRs had gathered in a conference room to discuss their First Contact with the Adens.

As they read the file describing the Adens, a race of beings standing forty feet tall, a sense of awe and nervousness filled the room. Karol said, *"Well, I didn't expect the Adens standing forty feet tall. That makes it rather difficult to sit at a table, show them documents, or receive documents."* Jank said, *"I think we should stay onboard the EFCV and communicate with Vid Chat. What if they step on us? We are flattened and dead or busted up. Yeah, I'm not going to the surface, nope, nope."*

Karol, her voice trembling, grabbed his arms and looked him in the eyes and said, *"Who will protect me? You must go, Jank, please! come with me."* Commander Turner walked into the conference room and asked, *"Who is your leader or chair for the group?"* Karol let go of Janks arms, but held his hand, *"I am Sir."*

"Oh, good, I'm Commander Turner, you and your group are vessel bound, you won't be going to the surface per order of GCM Synder, feel free to use our commons area and lunch hall. That is all, carry on." "Thank you, Commander." Turner bowed and walked away. Jonka said, *"Jank, let's review the file. You're done with it, right?" "Yes, well, no, but I did find an archive that will serve our purpose. I will send it to this view screen on the wall. Get comfy, everyone."* The narrator's voice was a famous actor.

Mysteries of the Universe

With your host Leonard

The Grigorians

Millions of cycles ago, an augmented humanoid named Bud, his actual name is not translatable, discovered a neighboring galaxy attached to the hub of the andromeda universe. Astro observers had speculated only one other arm could be attached to the hub. Bud used a state-of-the-art telescopic platform, which he modified to give both greater clarity and distance, located on a moon that orbited his home planet in the Milky Way galaxy.

Bud was astonished when he discovered the other three arms. He made several videos showing the other arms, and detailed videos of the closest arm to the Milky way. Astonished at his find he struggled to find an appropriate name for the galaxy. After much thought, he decided to ask his fellow astro scientists what to name the newly discovered galaxy.

The others deliberated and debated, which turned into a bitter and heated argument. Bud became frustrated over the arguing and named the galaxy after himself. Bud also discovered two planets within the neighboring galaxy. He named the first planet, a gas giant with thousands of active volcanos, Vulcan. The second planet, which was in close proximity and had reptile life forms on it, Grigori.

The life forms on planet Grigori were observed for many cycles by many types of scientists and ethologists. It was determined that the reptiles were a lower life form.

Bud didn't want to name the other two arms and felt other astro scientists should dedicate themselves to them. He fashioned a working model that resembled a pinwheel with four arms and used it as a visual aid at conferences when he discussed his discovery.

A group of augmented humanoids from planet Alnitak, within the Milky Way galaxy, had traded raw material to planets within the Pleiades planet group for a profit without the permission of the Galactic Council. Those who conducted such activities were considered Privateers or Pirates.

They heard of Bud's discovery and wanted to start mining operations on planet Grigori, however, they knew nothing about the planet. They hired an Exploration group of six augmented men and six augmented women from the Pleiades planet Eulgloohcs Prime.

They were well known for quickly gathering vital data about a planet without permission from the Galactic Council. They traded all information collected for materials, supplies, or technology. The Galactic Council branded such groups as Intelligence Pirates and advised harsh penalties for persons or parties involved with this activity.

Several Galactic Council members agreed planets have a right to explore their solar system and beyond so long as they do not invade, kill, or destroy any current occupants of a planet. The contract required the Explorers group to submit the first report to the augmented humanoids, who remained anonymous.

As Bud didn't make the exact coordinates of planet Grigori public, the only navigational information the Explorers had was a hand drawn map on a cocktail napkin. Upon arrival at planet Grigori, the explorer group orbited the planet to map its topography and survey areas to land on for soil samples.

The Explorers boarded their landing craft and descended to the planet's surface to gather soil samples. While on the surface, the group began a live broadcast to the anonymous augmented humanoids. They had been on the surface for ninety minutes and had collected soil samples of a rare mineral.

Several reptiles in the area noticed the group and surrounded them. The reptiles attacked the Explorers, ripped them apart, and ate them. When a reptile consumed a creature, the DNA from that creature was added to the reptile's DNA. The addition of DNA gave the reptile the ability to shape-shift into that creature's form and metabolism.

Like a puffer fish, a reptile's size could be increased in a matter of a second, from a boa snake to a one-hundred-foot dinosaur-like reptile. By expelling secretions, they reduced in size. The reptiles that had absorbed an Explorer's DNA shape-shifted into the form of that group member.

The other reptiles in the area were confused and chased them down and ate them, not realizing they were reptiles. This comedy of errors repeated itself until ten thousand reptiles could shape-shift into any member of the original Explorers group. Thinking exponentially, the convergence was fast, and at that point, the reptiles became Reptilians, now capable of space flight.

They had the Explorers group landing craft and used it to learn how to fly, they also had the orbiting space vessel to learn how to navigate space. Reptilians began to navigate to other planets in the Bud galaxy. As they landed on more planets to colonize, they became a space faring race and were always aware of the Milky Way galaxy.

It is assumed that the Reptilians dominated the entire arm of the Bud Galaxy and began to deplete their food source. After they landed on several planets in the Milky Way galaxy, the Reptilians were referred to as off-worlders from Planet Grigori, hence the Grigorians.

Their lifestyle was of consumption rather than of production or manufacturing. These technologies, along with trade goods and raw materials, weren't necessary for them.

Most of their vessels and equipment were from planets with intelligent life decimated by the Grigorians, who merely embraced the other's technology as their own.

The population of the Grigorians numbered in the millions within the Milky Way galaxy. They gave no value to life outside of their own race. Grigorians weren't racists, they ate everybody. The Grigorians had a common phrase: the larger the planet, the better. Most humanoid planets had art, music, ceremonial sites, rituals, and customs and were in balance with nature.

The Grigorians didn't have creative minds, they had engineering minds and a hive collective consciousness. On many levels, they were an impressive race of higher intelligence.

When the Grigorians attacked a normal size planet with humanoids, the defenders of that planet, along with forces from neighboring worlds, would join together to combat the Grigorians. Automated defensive systems successfully repelled some of the Grigorian's attacks preventing them from landing on the planet.

Direct combat with the Grigorians that successfully landed, happened primarily in remote areas of the planet and was always devastating for humanoids. The humanoids switched to a more concealed battle tactic and won more battles.

Most planets suffered a massive loss of life, as did the Grigorians before they retreated from the planet or conquered it. The conflict between Humanoids and Reptilians has been an ongoing semi-war up to the present cycle. As the Grigorians advanced with each generation, they became more human like and peaceful. The human form was preferred as it takes less energy to maintain.

The new generation of Grigorians discovered many benefits to the human form when procreation of children to expand the populace became necessary.

They also discovered procreation was pleasurable and only the female body had a cyclic pattern which allowed males to perform without the need of a mating season, increasing the population exponentially. Thank you for watching Mysteries of the Universe with your host, Leonard..."

Karol stood up and faced the other GCRs, *"Well, that's putting a whole new face on what we are here for. Thank you for the video, Jank."*

She rubbed her eyes and looked at the group, *"We are here for first contact with the Adens, and it appears they will have a negative view of augmented humanoids from the start. I'm at a loss as to what we say to the Adens. This discussion is now open for comments. Who wants to start?"*

The GCRs stared at Karol or looked away. Jank said, *" Well, there isn't going to be a negotiation with the Grigorians, so we don't have to worry about that. Let's go to the dining hall and regroup later."*

Expedi Force Vessels Arrive

Expedi Force vessels arrived in the Copernican solar system and established an orbit around Saturn. The EFCV and support vessels were the first to arrive. Envoys notified Aden, Mars, and Minertha Military Command that the Expeditionary Forces had gathered around Saturn, to recharge their vessel's main engines. After that the flotilla would start to their respective planets.

Mars Military Command (MMC) insisted four platoons of Mars Troopers remain stationed in all EF bases. Additionally, EF Command must share all intelligence gathered with MMC until the Expedi Force flotilla departs. Envoys notified GMF Command of this request.

Lt. Col. Nelson granted only intelligence that pertained to their planet would be shared. She acquiesced to the four platoons. EF Commanders added space to their base design outside the protected zone and notified MMC that the structures wouldn't accommodate their forty-foot-tall height.

Aden Military Command requested the EF Trooper vessels continue directly to Aden. Once in orbit, the vessels could siphon energy from the planet. Lt. Col. Nelson respectfully denied the request, citing protocol must be followed. They sent her an informational brochure.

The brochure showed flight paths around the planet to be used for vessel refueling and the items used for barter, *"Best little refueling station in the solar system, our restrooms are clean and inviting,"* was the top banner of the brochure.

Lt. Col. Nelson sent a reply, *"EF Troopers are not on holiday, however your planet will be listed as a tourist destination. Protocol must be followed."*

Minertha Military Command made no requests of GMF Command. They also included a travel brochure showing the historical sites on the planet.

Aboard PDV-109, anticipation filled the air as the Scientists and curious crew members gathered in the dining hall. All eyes were on the live broadcast from the probe, a crucial source of information about the unfolding events.

As the probe orbited at approximately sixty-thousand-miles, the Watchers hailed PDV-109 and requested Planet Registry Information, current course heading, and final destination coordinates. Porter looked at Nottap, *"Sir, a Watcher named Dnomyar is hailing us, and he wants our navigational information."*

Nottap walked over to the comms panel, *"Send it."* *"Aye, Sir."* Dnomyar replied, *"What is the purpose of the probe?"* Nottap replied, *"We launched the probe to observe the planet's surface should we encounter this race. You're welcome to connect to the probe for observation if you would like."*

Dnomyar accepted the offer and reported to GMF Command and EF Command his first observations of the Grigorians as they surrounded a capital city in a remote territory on Aden. He sent information to the Adens outlining his observations, and advised them to prepare for the attack. Dnomyar held back the connection information to the probe.

Dnomyar sent connection information to GMF Command and the EFCV Conflict Management Conference room. The Conflict Management Team (CMT) members are trained Negotiators, Arbitrators, Land Surveyors, Civil Engineers, Geologists and Ethologists.

Karol asked if the GCRs could sit in to observe. Her request was granted. They gathered in the conference room to observe as the Grigorians surrounded and prepared to attack the Capital city for the territory, Ninni.

Attack on Capital City Ninni

As the people from the remote areas around the city arrived, the city's population grew to one hundred twenty-five thousand people and fifty thousand animals. An alarm blared as Aden Military forces ushered the residents into the city for defense and shelter. Aden Troopers defended the city with the most modern weaponry for their planet.

The Grigorians wore uniforms that didn't display Military insignia and appeared to be Explorer group uniforms at first glance. As the Grigorians mingled, spotters noticed they had no weapons. Aden Military Command, Captain Cartwright, and Captain Cobber sent orders to the Troopers not to open fire unless fired upon.

The attack began when several Grigorians ran toward the defensive lines at a quick pace, the others followed. As the Grigorians closed in on the defensive line, the Grigorians leading the charge waved their arms, and the Grigorians behind them spread out. An Aden Trooper noticed this maneuver and shouted, " *They're flanking us, spread out."*

Lt. Woods radioed Captain Cartwright, *"LT2 to CC1, come in."* *"CC1 here." "Sir, they are flanking us, and we are having the platoons spread out." "Copy, CC1 out."* Troopers spread out along the defensive line. When it became apparent there were more Grigorians than Troopers, the defensive line Commanders defied orders. Lt. Woods sent orders, *"Defensive call and fire at will."*

Sgt. Foreman called out to his men, *"Defensive call, fire at will. Maintain your spacing."* As he walked down the line of Troopers, shouting the new order, the Grigorians ran toward them. The Grigorians were in a semicircle, spaced out in battle formation, side by side.

As the Grigorians closed in, the troops became nervous. Some platoons closed ranks, and large gaps developed in the defensive line between platoons. Captain Cobber, responsible for the second defensive line, radioed Lt. Wheeler. *"CC2 to LT2, come in." "LT2 here." "LT2, the first line has gaps. Move your platoons to fill them," "LT2 Copy."*

When the charging Grigorians reached blaster rifle range, they morphed into large sixty-foot-tall reptilians or eighty-foot-tall reptiles. Aden Troopers were stunned by the sudden appearance of reptilians and reptiles. Some fired in a panic, some fired at the feet of the reptiles, and some turned and ran away.

The Grigorians overran the first defensive line as platoons formed defensive semicircles. Troopers in the open scrambled for cover, other Troopers that stood their ground were torn to shreds or eaten whole. Troopers that had taken cover opened fire and kept firing until they ran out of ammunition. Requests for more ammunition went unanswered.

All they could do was find places to hide and watch the carnage. After the sounds of blasters faded to silence, they heard the sickening sound of flesh being ripped and chewed. Sgt. Foreman drew his knife and signaled his men to do the same. He gave the hand signal, *"Count of three, we charge."*

His platoon signaled a thumbs up. When both defensive lines fell, Captain Cartwright and Captain Cobber drove back to the city to inform the Citizens, *"Hide, everyone hide."*

At the defensive line slaughter, Reptilians expelled secretions and reduced to twenty-five-foot-tall Explorers. The reptiles expelled secretions and reduced to twenty-five-foot-tall iguanas or alligators, and they began to eat the dead Troopers. A Reptilian leader made a loud growl sound, and waved his arm in a circular motion. They turned and ran toward the city, the mass of the Reptilians followed.

Once they reached the city limits, they morphed back into Reptilians and reptiles. The reptiles smashed buildings, forcing people to run out. They were torn to shreds by the Reptilians, and some were eaten whole by the reptiles. A river of blood flowed down the streets and drained into the sewers and tunnel system. People hiding there, screamed in fear at the sight of the blood.

Reptiles expelled secretions and crawled into the sewers and tunnel system by squeezing through the grates. Screams of fear turned to screams of terror. Several Reptilians ripped the front doors off the school building and ran in. Children of all ages ran out the back. An older girl ran through the playground with a younger girl on her back.

A Reptilian caught them and slashed the older girl, and ate her leg. Another Reptilian ran after the younger girl and caught her. He held up the young one by her ankle, and watched as she squirmed and screamed in terror. The Reptilian staggered back as she screamed in its face.

It dropped the child and she quickly ran off. The Reptilian began to stagger as if dazed or inebriated, and walked back to the school building. On the EF command vessel, the GCRs stood up and walked out of the conference room, retching as they exited.

The Civil Engineers and Geologists hurled on the floor in front of their seats. Expedi Commanders sat in silence. The city was void of Aden life in roughly ninety minutes.

A Geologist asked a single question of the Expedi Commanders, "*If this was the first phase an attack by the Grigorians has been witnessed, how exactly has the Military tracked and killed thousands of Grigorians before this event?*" The question went unanswered as the EF Commanders stood up and walked away.

Sgt. Foreman

Sgt. Foreman and his platoon charged out of their hiding spot and saw reptiles, twenty-five feet tall, eating the dead Troopers. They sunk their bayonets into the sides of the reptiles. Sgt. Foreman sunk his knife into the neck of a reptile, and in an instant, it morphed into a forty-foot-tall reptilian.

As it changed shape, he grabbed the hair, and the head was decapitated. The reptiles killed by his platoon dissolved into puddles of black ooze.

Sgt. Foreman, still holding the severed head, looked at his men and noticed they had a shocked expression while they pointed at the head. He lifted the head to look at it as tentacles grew out of the neck. He dropped the head and punted it. The head spun end over end, landing with a hollow thud.

As they watched the severed head, the ears morphed into wings, and it flew away toward the city. Sgt. Foreman looked at the body as it dissolved into black ooze. He said to his men, "*We can kill them, listen up, we need to go to Command Central and tell them how.*"

Misclassification

GMF Command sent a message to the EFCV and CMT members. Operation SUEVAS has ended. Conflict status: MISCLASSIFICATION. The official narrative for *The Battle for Aden* reclassified the conflict as a *Cosmic Bug Infestation*. This title also closed the ongoing debate. GMF Command waited for an *all clear* from the Galactic Council before turning the flotilla around.

Lt. Col. Nelson called Lt. Col. Vanwyke and Major Whitman, requesting their presence in her office for a briefing on Operation Suevas. In the conference room on the EFCV, Carl Hanson, an Ethologist, looked at his fellow Ethologist Bernard Tanner and asked, "*How quickly can we evacuate the planet?*" Bernard answered, "*Not quickly enough.*" As the two sat and continued to watch the view screen, they watched reptiles expel secretions and reduced in size.

Bernard looked at Carl, "*Well, that's not at all humanoid, and that is a pretty gross sight.*" Carl shook his head, "*No, it's not humanoid, it's a bug, and I hope EF Troopers kill all those bugs without mercy.*"

Bernard's PDT vibrated, which startled him, and he jumped to his feet. Carl watched him and jumped up, yelling, "*What is it? What's wrong?*" Bernard chuckled as he said, "*Sorry, my PDT it ... anyway nothing's wrong ... this made me jumpy after watching that...Oh, look, GMF Command sent a message. "Operation Suevas is no longer active, all vessels and personnel will now cease operations and stand by for further instructions.*"

Bernard closed the message and looked at Carl, *"Are you good? You look ... oh wait ... there's more ... Misclassification of conflict, see attached reports, all vessels are required to hold on station at the main spaceport of Saturn for reassignment."* Bernard shrugged his shoulders, turned and walked toward the entryway.

Carl said, "*We what, leave? ... that's it? ... we're done? we turn tail and go home?"* Bernard called out over his shoulder, *"That's what it looks like, yes."* Carl replied in an angry voice, *"People died in front of our eyes, and we leave? We need to do something about this."*

Bernard reached the entryway and turned to look at Carl, "*Look at your PDT, this is now an aggressive insect problem, and watch where you step, yikes."* He turned and walked away.

Carl sat down and looked at the view screen. He leaned forward, covered his face with his hands, and began to cry, in his mind he knew Tami and her family had been killed. "*I met Tami, she was a sweet child. I'm so sorry, Tami ... I'm so sorry."* he said through his hands as he sobbed.

A Negotiator on the CMT, Kenneth, and an Arbitrator, Lena, walked over and sat next to Carl, one on each side. They placed a hand on his shoulder, and they began to sob.

Kenneth said, *"I recognized you from the group video call with the Aden people. You're Carl, right?"* Lena said, *"She was a sweet child, and as smart as they come. Come with us Carl, this is not over, but this is no longer a task for us."* Kenneth and Lena stood up, and helped Carl stand. The trio walked out the entryway.

Morphed

The Grigorians were now classified as a morphed bug life form. All diplomatic efforts ended. The conflict was moved from a military platform to an invasive BUG eradication platform. Like most BUGS that are hive or nest-like in nature, the Grigorians had collective intelligence and were well capable of defending whatever they took as theirs.

They didn't negotiate or compromise. *What's theirs is theirs, if it was yours, it is now theirs. What was there to discuss?* GCM Synder contacted Karol and gave her instructions to hold a conference on Saturn to rally support for a proposal she was pitching.

She felt it was time to take the Grigorian infestation seriously. She gave her a list of invitees. Also, a list of GCRs, who could assist her. The other GCRs were released from service for this assignment. Their parents sent transport to pick them up from Saturn.

Karol gathered the group and said, " *Jank, Jonka, Trop, and Nament, you're staying with me. Everyone else, GCM Synder has dismissed you, and transports are on the way to take you to your home worlds."* Jank asked, *"Why was I picked to stay?" "Janky, I asked her if you could stay with me, and she said "Sure."* Trop whispered to Jank in a musical tone, *"I hear wedding bells."*

New Orders

GCM Synder ordered GMF Command to keep the EF Command vessel and group at Saturn until further notice. Karol sent the invitees listed by GCM Synder invitations to the event on Saturn. The CMT and the GCRs departed the EF Command vessel headed for a pleasure palace on Saturn.

Representatives from the surrounding Worlds received the conference itinerary. It listed the introduction as a video of an attack on Aden.

First Topic: GMF Command reports outlining the seriousness of the morph bug lifeform and the threat it poses to all humanoid lifeforms.

Second Topic: Commercial bug eradication compared to a Military Operation bug eradication. Pros and Cons debate. A narrative written by GCM Synder, was included giving a slanted view to favor the military. The spin was subtle.

Final Topic: Funding and supplying a privatized Military Force for bug eradication using the PFPK format. (Pay For Proof of Kill).

Representatives from other worlds made reservations at hotels and spa resorts for rooms, and other accommodations. Media Influencers reported Saturn visitor centers, hotels and spas were filling up, and urged their viewers to be quick with making reservations. Karol also watched the Media Influencers, and was very excited and nervous.

"Jank, Should I wear a uniform or a formal dress, or a pants outfit? How's my hair? I should get it fixed up ... " Jank held her close and whispered in her ear, *"Be calm, I have something to show you, be calm."* He handed her a tablet and it showed the RSVP list was light. Karols shoulders dropped, and she flopped into a comfy chair.

She realized the Representatives were using the event as an excuse to party on Saturn. Most of the worlds in the quadrant were of average size, and they expressed concern that the five planets were moons. Several Media Influencers with millions of subscribers and high view hits per video, pushed the narrative that the small planets were moons of Jupiter.

They claimed an unknown object struck Jupiter twenty-five-thousand years ago causing the planet to shift seven degrees. This caused a great storm on Jupiter. The storm raged and grew until it covered the entire planet. Jupiter's gravitational pull decreased, and could no longer hold the moons in orbit.

They broke away, one moon every twelve years when Jupiter's orbit was at its closest point to the solar star. Galactic rules and laws don't cover moons, *"What happens on a moon, stays on a moon."* Moons are protected by the planets they orbit and follow the rules and laws of that planet. Karol said in a sad voice, *"My event is an excuse for debauchery, that's all it is."*

Review of Operation Suevas

Major Whitman and Lt. Col. Vanwyke arrived at Lt. Col. Nelsons's office at the same time. Vanwyke tapped on the door, she looked at him and he said, *"Charlie, you wanted to see us?"* *"Aye Sir, take a seat over in the side office. We need to watch this video. It's alarming. Our little planet problem has revealed a greater threat than we anticipated."*

The trio sat at a round table. Nelson clicked the remote and the video of the attack on Aden began. As the reptiles expelled secretions to enter the sewers, Major Whitman said, *"Okay, Charlie, I get the jest of it turn it off."*

Vanwyke rubbed his face with his hands, *"Sweet mother of Rah, the Expedi Forces are they on Aden now?"* *"Negative, Sir, they are holding on station at Saturn and waiting for the light air support vessel to arrive."* Major Whitman asked, *"Who has seen this video?"*

"Unknown Major, this video came from a probe launched by a Neiubo vessel PDV-109, no name on the registry, they are on a maiden voyage. A Watcher named Dnomyar sent this signal as a relay to GMF Command, Sir, it's gone viral."

Vanwyke said, *"Classify it right now, while we sit here, do it now."* Nelson leaped from her chair and went to her desk. After She finished typing, she swiveled her chair, *"Done, it's classified, but we don't know who else was connected to the feed."*

Major Whitman stood up, *"I need to go rinse my face."* Nelson pointed to a door, *"It's in there."* Whitman entered the restroom and closed the door.

Vanwyke and Nelson looked at each other as sounds of retching came from the restroom. Vanwyke said, *"That video is more than alarming Charlie, and as far as I know, Whitman has never been on the front line. You didn't give a proper warning."*

"Aye, Sir, I apologize. Sir, this problem is above my paygrade, I'm throwing it back into your court." "Aye, Charlie, I think I need to review this, and it sounds like you owe Whitman lunch or dinner if he gets an appetite. Not a good slide, Charlie, not a good slide." "Aye, Sir."

"Well, Charlie this is above my paygrade too. Gather what you have on this, and I will take it to the Generals and Admirals. Send the other files to my PDT. Finish your reports, and when Whitman comes out, send him back to the Academy. We are going to get a lot of questions out of this. I will contact fleet management and get a list of available vessels, we're going to need them. Before I go, any comments or questions?"

"Aye, Sir. I was reflecting on what could have happened if the rookies had made landfall. That would have been a lot of letters of condolences." "Aye, Charlie, we got lucky this phase, and so did they. It's best if you don't answer any questions directly, send them to me, and I will field them. Make note: This will be the last time we send rookies to any hot spot. We got lucky."

"Aye, Sir, we did." "Anything else?" "No, Sir." Vanwyke stood up, grabbed the file off Nelson's desk, and walked out the door.

Whitman stepped out of the restroom, his complexion was pale greenish. Nelson helped him over to the couch and had him lie down. She said, *"Apology for not giving you a good warning. I'll go get a Naval Doctor." "Thanks, and Charlie, my apology for the mess. I might have missed the bowl at first."*

Def Con One

On Aden, Military Command sent a planet-wide message to all bases and branches: *"Defensive Condition One."* All branches of the armed forces sent their top-level command to the Hexagon for a briefing. As each branch entered the auditorium, they sat in their appointed sections.

A trumpet blared out a cord, and they all stood up, placing a fisted hand on their hearts. The world Directors walked on stage, followed by Military Intelligence Command Officers. A voice announced, *"The Director of the United Territories."* Robert walked on stage from the right and stood in the middle.

He placed a fisted hand on his heart, bowed his head. He looked at the Officers and said, *"Be seated."* The sound of the Generals, their aides, the Armored Battle Division High Command, and their aides taking their seats was loud.

After the auditorium fell silent, Robert said, *"Men, the Galactic Council bureaucrats won't be sending any of their Troopers. They say this is a planet problem, and we have a Bug Problem. It was useless to contact them. We can't wait, and we shouldn't wait, for another attack.*

That said, I'm open to accepting help from anyone willing to help. Being free on these lands, we, the People of Aden, have always maintained Peace by Strength. As a rule of the land, we have always helped each other during phases of hardship. Ninni, the capital city of the Orado territory was a slaughter house."

Robert walked to the left side of the stage and looked at the Army Generals, *"The Reptilians have taken Ninni, and I want you to take it back. Make them pay, no prisoners, no survivors, I want black ooze to fill the sewers. I authorize you to take extreme measures and Do Not Accept a Surrender.*

Take Ninni back, that is your order. The only restriction is, leave half of the Army back should we face a Last Stand Scenario. Tell the Troopers they must fight to the last man and any Trooper that runs will be killed, shot down as a cowardly worthless dog. Come back victorious, or don't come back. You know what I'm conveying with that statement."

Robert walked to the right side of the stage and looked at the Armored Battle Division High Commanders. He cleared his throat and said, *"Send two mechanized divisions and four artillery divisions and surround Ninni. Nobody comes out, nobody gets by your firing line, including Troopers who may run from battle, nobody gets by the firing line.*

The Army will contact you to advance on Ninni after they have killed all the Reptilians and reptiles. If the Army is not successful, full barrage on Ninni. Leave no building standing and destroy all infrastructure buildings, power plants, storehouses, and transportation ports, all of it."

He walked to the center of the stage and said, *"I know what I am ordering you to do is hard, and goes against your morality, but it must be done. We do this because we can't allow the Reptilians to occupy our city after they viciously killed our citizens.*

They offered no quarter, they gave no mercy, men, women, children, livestock, and pets. They ate the cats, they ate the dogs, they ate them, the pets. They chased down the pets, what army does that? They slaughtered all life horrifically, and our new enemy now occupies the city.

We didn't ask for this fight, but we will end it. They set the tone of this conflict. Our people had no weapons to defend themselves because they turned in their blasters during the mandatory voluntary redemption law signed by the former Director of the United Territories.

They were not military soldiers, they would have complied or surrendered if given the chance. Our people shall be avenged. So, we will do unto them as they have done unto us. Leave no survivors, kill them all, avenge our people. You all have intel on Sgt. Foreman and his platoon, brave men, all of them.

Bayonets and knives, if slicing and stabbing is how we need to kill them, that is what you need to do. This attack ends here, no further, no prisoners, no mercy. You will be the heroic men who avenge the people. Do not come back without a total victory. This entire planet will be saved and our people will be avenged and all of you. All of you are ... our saviors. That is all, please stand for the ceremonial closing and prayer."

PDV-109

As the EFCV and flotilla waited for the air support vessel to arrive at Saturn, PDV-109 arrived in the solar system. The plotted course had them passing between Aden and Jupiter. The Navigation Officer aboard the EFCV noticed their arrival.

The EFCV, under SOP (*Standard Operational Procedure*), hailed PDV-109 and requested Planet Registry Information, the purpose of travel with final destination coordinates, and the current course heading.

Porter turned to face Nottap, "*Sir, the EFCV is hailing us.*" "*Aye, Hold reply.*" Nottap stood up and asked the bridge crew a single question, "*Go or Stay?*" When nobody answered the question, Nottap shouted more forcefully, "*Go or stay!?*"

If they only had known how galactically impactful that question was, they might have altered course and merely kept going. The EFCV repeated the hail and locked onto PDV-109 with a targeting beam. Porter responded to the hail with the requested information.

Crawford heard the targeting lock tone, he stood up and went to the comms panel, connected, and said, "*PDV-109 First Officer to EFCV, what is the purpose of the targeting beam? We are not military or hostile. However, we will defend ourselves. Do you copy?*"

The EFCV's response was swift and direct, "*Hold on station for a crew verification and vessel search.*" Crawford disconnected from the comms panel and urgently called out to Nottap, "*Commander, the EFCV has target locked us, and ordered us to hold on station for crew verification and a vessel search.*"

Nottaps command was firm and decisive, "*Pilots, hold on station, standard station keeping, and lower shields to minimum.*" Logan and Windstorm's response was an immediate, "*Aye Sir.*"

Bug Eradication

Gov of Nav Corp was also connected to the live broadcast from the probe. The Gov of Nav Corp opened a comms link to PDV-109. Porter urgently called out, *"Commander, The Gov of Nav Corp is calling you."* The Gov of Nav Corp, with a tone of gravity, advised Nottap and Crawford to offer a first bid and contract to the occupants of Aden for a bug eradication of their planet.

Nottap, fully aware of the significance of this task, reminded the Gov of Nav Corp, they had a limited crew on board. Crawford assisted the EF Troopers with crew verification and the vessel search as Nottap remained on the bridge.

As the Gov of Nav Corp had expressed to Nottap, the planet was the size of a "*grain of sand, eight thousand miles in diameter, how many could there be?"* which made this a "*Little Side Job"* on the way to their final destination, *"in and out operation, quick and easy."*

Each Department Manager aboard PDV-109 received instructions from the Gov of Nav Corp of this *"Little Side Job."* Their task was to assist Nottap in writing a first bid proposal and contract for a bug eradication service. The Gov of Nav Corp ended the communication by saying, *"What could go wrong?"*

The department managers went to the bridge and advised Nottap of the instructions from the Gov of Nav Corp to assist him with the contract.

He stood up and asked rhetorically, "*We aren't bug exterminators, we build planets, and transport people, don't they know that? Did they forget that? What could go wrong? They said that?"* Nottap shook his head, walked to his command chair, and sat down.

He began to search the database and found "*How to Negotiate a Contract and Win.*" The Department Managers slowly step back toward the lift. Without looking at them, he said, "*The lift is locked, so go to a data terminal and start reading.*" Nottap and the Managers, strategizing their approach, used a boiler plate contract which was used by service providers on Neiubo.

They made meticulous modifications to fit their unique situation. The contract, if accepted, would provide Neiubo with twenty cycles of a specific metal found on Aden, and provide the Adens with a bug free planet. They added standard provisions that are common in Galactic contracts.

Nottap, confident in their strategy, sent the finalized version of First Bid offer and contract to the Gov of Nav Corp for approval. He requested comments. Gov of Nav Corp sent a message, "*Excellent Commander, send it to The Director of the United Territories Robert.*" Nottap sent a reply, "*Thank you. We all helped to construct the contract the same way we help each other build a planet, which is what we do.*"

Gov of Nav Corp replied, "*Good teamwork. You and the crew of PDV-109 are granted authority to negotiate for The Gov of Nav Corp. Keep in mind the phrase, "For the good of Nav Corp." Keep me informed and notify me if they need special provisions, Gov of Nav Corp out.*"

Nottap muttered to himself, "*I was being sarcastic.*" He looked at the Department Managers and said, "*Gov of Nav Corp approved our First Bid offer and contract, which I'm sending to, Robert, The Director of the United Territories. He also gave us authority to negotiate for the Gov of Nav Corp, which means we are all here until we have a signed contract, so stop looking bored. We could be here for a while.*" All the Department Managers leaned back in their chairs and groaned or muttered a complaint.

We Accept your offer

Robert sent a message to Nottap and the Governance of the Navigators Corporation. The message read, "*As the Director of the United Territories on Aden I accept your offer on behalf of the people of Aden, you may start work immediately,*" attached was a signed contract.

Robert sent a copy of the contract to the Galactic Council with a note attached, "*We, the people of Aden, request your EF vessels remain in the solar system should unexpected problems arise.*" Galactic Council forwarded the contract and note to GMF Command.

Lt. Col. Nelson sent a message to Robert, "*Your formal request for Expedi Force vessels to stand by is denied. Our GMF units cannot participate in nonmilitary activities, however, Galactic Council Representatives are currently holding a video conference from Saturn, which may give Expedi Forces in your area extended authority to assist your planet. I will keep you informed, End of Transmission.*" After reading the message Robert muttered, "*I won't hold my breath.*"

The standard procedure for Bug Eradication required relocation of the occupants on the infested planet temporarily. Launch a series of missiles to predetermined locations in the area of the cosmic bugs' hives or nests. The missiles had a specific form of gamma radiation variant in the payload. This would kill bugs quickly as it contained a cascade element designed to attack specific DNA.

The gamma radiation variant would dissipate after one rotation without leaving residue. Once dissipated, the residents could reoccupy the planet, which is no big deal, as this was done throughout the galaxy by trained and qualified exterminators. Most occupants of planet Aden were transported off to Mars or Minertha by military vessels, private vessels, or cargo vessels.

Copernican Solar System

Inner Planets

Zeus

Mercury

Venus

Minertha

Mars

Aden

The planets were coming into alignment which made the round-trip flights short. Nottap ordered five Olympus Wrath Landing vessels to Aden to assist with the relocation operation. The Olympus Wrath Landing vessels were piloted by Launcher Crew members, former GMF Troopers who had served as Pilots during their tenure. Their recognition of service also excluded them from the crew verification process.

On the EFCV the Navigations Officer noticed the Wrath Landing Vessels preparing to depart PDV-109 as the space dock doors opened. He placed a target lock on the Wrath vessels and sent a message. *"Stand down or we will fire."* The message flashed across the navigation screen on the Wrath vessels. The Pilots of the Wrath Landing group turned off their engines and placed their hands on the ceiling of their cockpits. An emergency alarm blared on the bridge of PDV-109, and a red light flashed from the navigation panel.

Nottap and IT Department Manager Babbage responded to the navigation panel and reset the alarm. Babbage looked at the view screens and noticed the Pilots with their arms up. He pointed to a view screen and asked Nottap, "*Sir, why are they doing that?*" Nottap looked at the view screen and transmitted a message to the EFCV.

"*PDV-109 Commander to EFCV, the vessels preparing to depart are going to Aden to assist with the evacuation of the planet, but I forgot to ask for permission. Please release our landers from target lock, we are not military or hostile.*"

After a lengthy delay, the EFCV responded with "*Permission granted*" and turned off the target lock. Nottap radioed the Pilots of the Wrath Landing group, "*Commander to Wrath Landing Group, apologies, I forgot to ask for permission first, you're free and clear to launch, and again, apologies about that.*"

The Wrath Landing Group Leader chuckled, "*That's alright, sir. SNAFU, we will be departing as soon as we get clean uniforms. Wrath Landing Group Leader Out.*" Nottap muttered, "*Snafu? Snafu? Wonder what that means,*" as he looked at Babbage. Babbage smiled at Nottap, shrugged his shoulders, and returned to his seat.

Congratulations

The sound of the lift as it opened startled everyone on the bridge. "*Why did you lock the lift?*" asked Crawford as he stepped out and walked to his Command Chair. He looked around and noticed a fatigued and panicky look on all the Department Managers' faces, "*Oh, I see.*"

As he sat down in his command chair, sounds of heavy sighs of relief filled the air, "*Good to see you too.*" he muttered as he picked up his PDT. Nottap called out, "*You're all dismissed from the bridge, and thank you for your help. Have your people start working on this assignment.*"

The Department Managers began packing themselves into the lift one at a time. Crawford and Nottap noticed the sound of grunting and muffled voices. They stood up and faced the lift. They watched as the Managers contorted themselves into the lift.

Crawford called out, "*Okay guys ... relax now ... there are only three on the lift.*" As the lift doors closed, he said, "*They actually all fit, I wouldn't have guessed it was possible.*"

Nottap chuckled and said, "*Aye, that was amazing how they did that, have you ever seen the video on tubulars' mating?*" "*Um...No, Sir ... I think I would have remembered that.*" "*Well, First Officer, that's what it looks like, exactly, minus clothes and arms .... Legs ... otherwise, exactly.*"

Crawford looked at Nottap, smiled and asked, "*Exactly, Sir?*" "*Aye, First Officer, exactly.*" Crawford turned, walked to his command chair and sat down. He laughed as he muttered, "*Exactly.*"

He picked up his PDT, and looked at Nottap, "*Congratulations on your contract, Sir.*" "*Thanks, I had help,*" Crawford smiled, "*I see that.*" Expedi Troopers had completed the crew verification process and released the crew to return to duty.

As the bridge crew returned, Crawford looked at Tracker, "*Nav, alter course to establish an orbit around Aden, and send the Pilots the new plotted course and delete the current course. Copilot tends to wander in his thoughts.*"

Tracker laughed. "*Aye, Sir, I never heard it put that way before, but I'm glad you noticed.*" Tracker sat down and began to set a course, he turned toward Crawford, "*Sir, are we orbiting above the water membrane or beneath it?*" "*Good question. Get us there and on approach, we will get a better view as I'm not sure we would fit under it.*" "*Aye, Sir.*"

Crawford reviewed information about Aden on his PDT. He noticed Nottap had posted on the vessel log that he had sent the Olympus Wrath group to assist with evacuating the Aden populace.

He sent a message to the Olympus Wrath Landing Group Leader, "*First Officer to Wrath Group Leader, offer to transport supplies or other cargo as the Aden people are forty feet tall and will not fit in the Olympus, standing by for acknowledgment.*"

A message returned: "*SNAFU ... acknowledge Wrath Landing Group Leader,*" he chuckled and scrolled his PDT looking for videos on tubulars' mating.

Grigorian Scouts

The Grigorians, now considered a cosmic bug with space travel capabilities, noticed the evacuation of the Aden people. They watched several vessels travel to Mars and Minertha. They understood their food source was being depleted and dispatched scout units from their collective to Mars and Minertha. The planets were in close orbit and that allowed the Grigorians' vessels to remain undetected.

Galactic Military vessels that could monitor their activity were in orbit around Saturn as they waited to depart the solar system. Grigorians planned to slip in with regular traffic going to Mars or Minertha and use the traffic as cover, protecting them from detection. The Mars group leader was The Wise One.

He was over ten thousand Grigori years old, and his natural state was a turtle. The Minertha group leader was Isolep, who was eight thousand Grigori years old, and her natural state was an Osaur.

Both leaders were united in their mission, following the same orders and directives. Their goal was clear: find a safe location with natural camouflage or concealment and a constant or replenishing food source. Send scrambled radio reports back every morning rotation, ensuring their communication is secure.

Each group had thirty members, and the Group Leaders handpicked the members. The group trained together, revealing their strength and weaknesses. They shared a kill, taking bites of the prey, this gave them the ability to morph into the same form if necessary. Top priority for scout groups is observe and report. Second priority is stealth, avoiding contact and conflict, this would ensure the survivability of the group.

Classified

In the science section of PDV-109, the Scientists gathered to discuss how to proceed. They agreed that not a single Scientist had any experience with such an assignment. Science Department Manager Gazou entered the laboratory conference room and called for his Junior Science Officer, Sufjan.

He looked at Sufjan and said, "*JSO 10, Bring everyone in here. We need to go over this assignment, and I want everyone on the same page. Exclude the Science staff assigned to the bridge.*" "*Aye, Sir.*"

As Planetary Scientists this assignment was as foreign as a new language. Gazou walked to a data terminal, sat down, and began to search the database. He looked for information on bug eradication and found "*How to eradicate bugs, by Elmer and coauthor Dafee.*" and several "*Do it yourself*" videos by the Warrens Brothers, none of which matched the parameters of their assignment.

"*This little side job will equal a big pain in the neck,*" he muttered as he continued his data search. Scientists had gathered in the conference room, Gazou said, "*We need to keep as much information as practical "classified" as this is the first phase anyone throughout the galaxy has attempted to conduct an operation of this size. This could be valuable.*"

A Scientist said, "*Well, how exactly will we do that?*" Gazou paused for a moment and said, "*That is why we are all here, to figure this out. If we are successful, we could get a big fat bonus.*"
The Scientist said, "*A probe is too small, so I guess we can modify one of the 18-gram impact projectile second-stage units.*"

Another Scientist stood up and said, *"How will we get the second stage to our lab and side-step protocol? We can't do that we don't know how."* He looked at the scientist and said, "*That's why we are all here, to figure this out."*

As the Scientists looked at each other and muttered or whispered, Gazou said, *"What we need is crewmen we can trust or somehow manipulate into helping us get the second stage to our lab. RSO12, you're a back-alley dweller, you must have connections. That's your assignment. Get that second stage here. The rest of you pull up the schematics and study it."*

The 18-gram Projectile

The Scientists aboard PDV-109 specialized in various fields. Their assignment for the maiden voyage was to collect elements used in the formation of a planet. None had experience with an endeavor such as this. After several short meetings, the scientists decided the best option was to confer with exterminators on performing a Bug Eradication.

Gazou again reminded the scientists their efforts are "*Classified*" and suggested they should find information in the database or watch a few "*How to*" videos. As the scientists began to work on the schematic to modify the impact projectile, it occurred to them engineering fabrication and projectile specialists have access to their database.

After several meetings, they decided their best option for modifying an 18-gram impact projectile without notice of Command or other Department Managers would be to modify it in sections. They mislabeled several files instead of using one main file that held the schematic.

Eighteen grams was the smallest impact projectile aboard PDV-109. The 18-gram nuclear weight payload was 10 grams too large for this little planet. Gazou made calculations to fire the projectile in a glancing blow. He also approved the modifications to the gamma radiation load, adding a variant to alter its lethal effect.

The projectile was modified to generate a faster than normal disintegration rate after delivery impact. The Impact Projectile now had an 8-gram nuclear payload. However, the delivery system's gravity weight remained the same: 18 grams.

Dimensions of the 18-gram impact projectile are 1,454 feet overall height. The second stage, with the impact head, is 485 feet with a single engine with four fins set for a right spin spiral.

The main body, first stage, is 969 feet with two engines, four fins set for a left spin spiral, and a launch velocity of 186,000 miles per second *(Velocity kills)*.

The impact would produce a crater seventeen miles deep and eighteen hundred miles in diameter. For average size planets the crater is not noticeable from space. For Aden it will be a pronounced crater and resemble a pock-mark on the face of the planet. As part of standard protocol, all the equations were to be checked and verified by each department manager and the Command staff.

A test fire was also part of standard protocol procedure, using an inert material in the payload, which would burn up somewhere in the Aden atmosphere after it pierced the water membrane.

As Scientists modified the 18-gram impact projectile second stage and impact head. They excluded the first stage during their flight path velocity calculations. The test fire was scheduled as "*bypass*" by Gazou.

Engineering Manager Schmidt had been waiting for the Scientists to submit a copy of the build schematics when he noticed the test fire was listed as "*bypass.*" He called Projectile Specialist Manager Newsome and asked, *"Have you received the schematics from the scientists yet?"* Newsome replied, "*No, nothing yet, but let me know when you receive them, I'm putting my people off rotation for a while." "Will do."*

Launcher Manager Yeldarb walked into Schmidt's office and asked, "*Did you notice the "bypass" on the schedule?*" "*I did.*" "*Well, let's go have a talk with the Scientists. My guys are starting to play football, and you know what that means.*"

Schmidt rubbed his jaw, "*Aye, I do, it's still a little tender,*" Yeldarb chuckled. As the two were about to walk out the door of engineering, three Scientists walked in, and the two groups almost knocked into each other. "*Hello there!*" shouted a Scientist.

Yeldarb chuckled, "*It's Good to almost bump into you. We were on our way to the Science Department. Let's step back in.*" The group walked over and stood by a data terminal. Schmidt and Yeldarb were expecting the Scientists to display the build schematics.

Schmidt turned on the screen when a Scientist said, "*We're here to inform you both we have configured an 18-gram impact projectile, and it is ready to launch.*" Yeldarb asked, "*The test fire launch?*" before the Scientist could answer, Schmidt asked, "*What do you mean, <u>configured an 18-gram impact projectile</u>?*"

The Scientist looked at Yeldarb, "*Sir, the test fire will not be conducted as all calculations have been made. It will be a live launch.*" The Scientist looked at Schmidt, "*Sir, this is a little <u>side job</u>, and we will not spend phase configuring two 18-gram impact second stage projectiles.*"

Schmidt asked, "*What do you mean, "configuring two 18-gram impact projectile second stage units? And when did you get the second stage? Explain to me what you did.*"

The Scientists called Gazou and asked him to report to Engineering as the two managers had questions they couldn't answer. Gazou walked into the engineering section and stated, "*The test fire will be bypassed, we have positive results, the projectile is ready for a live launch, and we are done here.*"

Schmidt, again, objected to the decision to "*bypass*" the test launch, he stated, "*The two are not the same in build or function, and how did your people get the 18-gram projectile second stage to the science department?*"

Gazou said in a haughty voice, "*Have you been to the science department?*" "*Um, well, no.*" "*Well, it would be pointless for me to explain.*"

We Need a Test Fire

Yeldarb stepped up to Gazou and asked in a low menacing voice, *"Have you been to the sick bay?"* Schmidt stepped between them, *"Allow me to show you our concern."*

Schmidt displayed the probe and the 18-gram impact projectile on the same screen. The probe is a sleek, single-engine, three-finned cylinder. The contents would fold out after it established an orbit around the planet. The contents included a solar panel and a signal broadcast dish.

The 18-gram impact projectile is a robust two-stage rocket with two engines per stage with four fins per stage, lower and upper. Attached to the upper stage is the impact explosive head with payload canister. Inventory showed PDV-109 had four in stock.

18-gram impact projectiles are used to clear volcanic debris from a planet when volcanic activity has stopped and cooled. After impact fungi, which is in the payload canister, is injected into the planet to start plant life. Engineering Fabrication could also build a custom impact projectile.

Yeldarb side stepped Schmidt and looked at Gazou. He said, *"You want us to shoot a rocket at a tiny piece of glass and graze it? We need to build an appropriate-sized projectile."*

Schmidt stated, *"I agree with his analogy, it's valid and to the point. What you're attempting to do can be accomplished with a custom build projectile. If you continue in this overkill fashion a test fire should be scheduled."*

With a smug voice, Gazou looked at Yeldarb and said, *"I will speak plainly. Your objection is noted. However, the test fire will not be conducted. ALL calculations have been made. Care to look at them? You can read a velocity data report, can't you?"*

Yeldarb squinted his eyes as he glared at Gazou and, in a low growling voice, said, "*Head or Gut?*" Schmidt stepped between them and looked at Gazou. "*What I'm saying is, the probe passed through the water membrane, and your calculations show only the second stage passing through the water membrane. We need a test fire.*"

Gazou said in a smug voice, "*Noted. However, the test fire will not be conducted. ALL CALCULATIONS HAVE BEEN MADE! WE'RE DONE HERE!*" Schmidt stepped back, looked at Yeldarb, and yelled, "*Gut!*"

Aden Representatives

The three planets, Minertha, Mars, and Aden, had a thick water membrane around the planet, which acted like, and from the ground looking up, resembled an ocean. The computer models provided by Gazou and Sufjan, checked out, and conditions were *"good for launch."*

After final preparations and checklist verification, the projectile was loaded into the launcher. The targeting computer displayed the meticulously calculated flight path of the projectile to the impact zone, the estimated debris spread of the gamma radiation variant, and the projected time for total bug eradication.

As the launch of the projectile drew near, representatives of the Aden people, from each territory, were eagerly invited to attend a gathering on PDV-109 to witness the meticulous operation and prep work for the launch. This was customary, and it assured clients the planet would be safe to return to, *or part of the sales job, whichever.*

Crawford had Engineering Crewmen reshape the visitors section to accommodate the Adens, who stood forty feet tall. Crew Services informed the galley to provide light refreshments and finger food suitable for the Adens. As the Aden Representatives arrived on PDV-109, many curious crewmen entered the visitor's section, waved hello, looked around, and leave.

Other crewmen preferred to peer off the balcony section, as it provided a more discreet advantage. Yeldarb walked onto the balcony and noticed one of his Launcher crewmen. The crewman was standing by the rail looking down at a female Aden Representative. Yeldarb stood next to him, also looking at the female Aden Representative. He said, *"She's forty feet tall and most likely has a lifestyle above your paygrade, so enough gawking for now, Trooper. Return to the Launcher Section."* The crewman sighed and said, *"Aye, Sir."*

Schmidt and Newsome walked onto the balcony and stood next to Yeldarb. The three looked down at the crowd. Newsome said to Yeldarb, "*I heard what happened in engineering, and I'm so jealous of you right now.*"

Yeldarb chuckled and looked at Schmidt, "*You spreading rumors?*" Schmidt chuckled, "*It ain't a rumor if it's the truth, and First Officer denied our request to suspend the live launch.*" Yeldarb sighed, "*Aye, I respect First Officer but can't understand why he trusts the Scientists.*"

Newsome looked at Yeldarb and said, "*Hang on there, those Scientists are the reason we all have been successful in the past, and not to mention it was Scientists that saved many PDV crews that found themselves in a tough spot, so go easy on the Scientists. It's their manager who's a real piece of work.*"

"*Aye, well, I didn't certify the launch, if anything goes wrong it's on that, piece of work.*" Schmidt said, "*I'm still curious how they were able to get an impact projectile explosive head to their lab to modify. Appears to me Commander and First Officer are not asking obvious questions.*" Yeldarb's voice was tinged with a hint of worry, "*As for the launch, I'm sure it will be a perfect launch. My guys are well trained and we don't have to worry about that piece of work for a while.*"

The three chuckled while looking down at the crowd. Nottap entered the visitors section and walked up the ramp to the elevated stage. He raised his hands and said, "*Can I have your attention please, thank you.*" Yeldarb tapped Newsome and Schmidt on the arm and made a motion to leave.

As the trio left the balcony, they heard Nottap say, "*Welcome honored guests from Aden ...* "Newsome asked, "*You guys want to go to the galley and get a drink?*" "*Sure ... yup.*"

Projectile Away

The populace on Mars and Minertha were given live broadcast information to observe the event from auditoriums set up to provide a festive atmosphere. The impact time was ninety seconds after launch for safety reasons, should an error occur, and it required the self-destruct option.

Aden Representatives on PDV-109 held hands in a semi-circle as they stood and faced a view screen that showed their home world with the Planetary Developers logo underneath it. They lifted their faces and began to pray to their deity, the source of all they were and their provider.

On Minertha, the Adens had gathered at an outdoor amphitheater with a large screen. People from both planets enjoyed the open festival the community set up for the event. Vendors trading for food gave the Adens plates of food and tumblers full of drink without accepting any trade items.

Vendors trading for souvenir tee shirts gave all Adens folk who walked by a colored tee shirt, on the front was the hand drawn picture Tami made of her family standing in front of their house.

On Mars, the Adens were ushered into an airship hanger by Military Command. They had no refreshments. A large view screen covered the back wall, and chairs were placed facing the screen and separated, which discouraged conversation. The Adens felt uncomfortable with the surroundings, as the bleak walls and gray floor gave a sense of oppression.

Launcher Tech Dodson finished his prelaunch checklist and announced, *"Launching projectile in ten short phases."* The crowds shouted the countdown as the numbers flashed on the view screens, showing Aden. *"Four, three, two, one, LAUNCH, Projectile away!"* the crowds shouted and cheered.

Return data showed the projectile was traveling at a higher velocity for its form, but within the flight path. As the projectile approached the outer atmosphere, the explosive tip activated, it was set to explode upon impact. The water membrane sensed the projectile approaching and constricted, turning to ice.

As the projectile broke through the ice, it turned at a sharp angle. It now spiraled toward the center of the planet, "*Projectile off course, Projectile off course*," a computer voice blared. A loud bell rang and the computer voice blared, "*Correct course immediately*" several times.

Dodson ran over to the Projectile control panel and pushed the abort button. The computer voice, now joined by a buzzing noise, said more urgently, "*Abort! Abort! Abort!*" A loud shrill alarm now joined the blare of the computer voice, adding to the chaos.

Dodson, his voice trembling with panic, yelled back "*I did that, why didn't it blow up? Computer voice command, execute self-destruct sequence now.*" The computer voice, now calm but with an underlying sense of urgency, responded, "*Auto self-destruct initiated, Auto self-destruct initiated, Self-destruct signal non-responsive, Self-destruct signal non-responsive.*"

Dodson, now in a state of sheer panic, frantically pushed control buttons on the projectile control panel. Return data showed *Communications disconnected.* He ran to the Launcher Control panel and switched on the intercom system to the bridge. In a high-pitched, trembling voice, he screamed "*First Officer what should I do? Are you there? First Officer?*"

Crawford, his voice filled with a mix of concern and determination, yelled out "AYE, *I'm here! I hear you!*" Crawford said in a calm, firm voice, "*Where are you?*" "*I'm at the Launcher Control panel.*"

Crawford said in a calm firm voice, "I *need you to go to the projectile control panel and retransmit the self-destruct signal." "Aye, Sir, I did that, and nothing happened."*

"Aye, listen, steady yourself, keep transmitting the self-destruct signal, and wait for orders. Are you clear?" Dodson replied, in a calm yet excited voice, *"Aye, Sir."* Time to impact was unknown due to the water membrane as it constricted and turned to ice, which bounced all signals into space. On Mars, a collective gasp was heard as the live broadcast, and all monitors went blank.

Nottap asked Tracker, *"Did it self-destruct?"* *"Negative, Sir, it is currently heading for the planet's surface, off the center of mass."*

The Launcher crew watched the impact projectile from the launcher section and witnessed the projectile slam into the planet. They covered their mouths with their hands to muffle screams and looked at each other with panic in their eyes. They began to run around the launcher bay, they were looking for a place to hide. Several remote unmanned observation posts still active on Aden sent a live broadcast on a military channel, not provided to the populace.

This channel was viewed by Tracker, GMF Command, EF Command and Gov of Nav Corp. It gave a ground view perspective for this unprecedented event as no planet this small had under gone an operation of this magnitude. As they watched, the projectile slammed into the planet. A crater was formed with fractures that grew in an instant.

As a fracture raced toward the observation post the screen went blank. The probe that was launched earlier to observe the planet's surface was in orbit on the back side of Aden, under the water membrane. The probe showed an unknown object as it exited the planet and water membrane at high velocity.

As the onboard computer sent estimated flight path and velocity data, the probe signal was lost, the last transmission showed an impact alert with the current location of the probe.

Several vessels that orbited Aden outside the water membrane reported an object had exited the planet and water membrane in the western region, and large chunks of the planet followed. The flight path showed the object was headed toward Mars.

Vessels that orbited Aden outside the water membrane left the area as fast as possible as part of the planet, and the water membrane blew out from the exit hole. The water membrane exploded in a slow-motion fashion. Many of the smaller vessels were destroyed, as was the Olympus Wrath Landing group.

Debris from the exploding planet and water membrane were headed toward PDV-109. Nottap shouted, "*Pilot, enter the nearest wormhole to Saturn and hold on station upon arrival.*"

Crawford jumped up from his command chair and shouted, "*Belay that order, Pilot, get us out of the way of incoming debris. Nav Plot a course that will put us between Minertha and Mars, we cannot abandon the people of Aden.*" Nottap shouted, "*Agreed, execute those orders.*" "*Aye, Sir.*"

Navigators Flying Cross

PDV-109 accelerated with a lurch, throwing Crawford back into his command chair, and he landed on his side. Nottap chuckled as Crawford adjusted himself. *"I wasn't going to abandon them, I needed a phase to think."* Crawford grinned at Nottap, *"We don't have that much phase, Sir. Comms, sound General Quarters." "Aye, Sir, General Quarters."*

Porter pushed a button on his control panel. A loud bell rang from the PA speakers, which indicated to the crew that they needed to secure themselves wherever they stood or sat.

Logan said, *"Hold tight, the ride will be rough."* Logan looked at Windstorm, *"You take the engine control, and I'll navigate." "Aye, copy that."* They flew PDV-109 as if it were an Olympus Wrath Landing vessel, with quick and sharp maneuvers. As PDV-109 turned left and right, ascended, and descended, crewmen began to slide across the deck.

At one point, it completed a serpentine maneuver so erratic the bridge crew floated off their chairs and were pushed back down. Logan noticed larger chunks approaching PDV-109 at high velocity and yelled, *"Salmonidae forty-two!" "Aye, copy that,"* yelled Windstorm. Logan made several quick turns and flew between the large chunks. He noticed buildings and animals on some of the larger chunks.

Windstorm slowed the PDV by activating the reverse thrusters, and reducing the forward engines. This made the crew lunge forward. He pushed the negative yaw button, and the PDV dropped under a large hunk. Crewmen became weightless, their feet floated off the deck as they hung onto side rails or consoles.

"Full throttle!" yelled Windstorm as he turned off the reverse thrusters and pushed the forward engines to maximum power.

A jolt backward, and crewmen were pinned to their seats, slid across the deck to the opposite wall or landed on the deck with a whump. As the PDV followed the plotted course set by Tracker, Windstorm slowed to normal velocity. Nottap called out, "*Secure from General Quarters.*" "*Aye, Sir, Secure from general quarters.*" Porter pushed a button on his control panel.

Tracker said, "*Watch where you step, I think my heart flew out of my chest.*" Porter called out, "*My chair got intimate with me. Yikes Pilot, you said rough ride, not death-defying.*" Crawford called out, "*As you were, check your systems. Comms, get a status report from all departments, and notify the Medics to set up triage stations on all decks. Notify the Medics in sick bay to activate the auto-nurses. Commander, did my left eye fly outta my head?*"

Nottap laughed, "*I think my stomach is on the ceiling, yikes Pilot, how many barter tickets do you charge for that wild ride?*" Logan gave Windstorm a side glance with a prankish smile, Windstorm winked at Logan. Windstorm called out, "*You okay back there, First Officer.*"

A writing fob struck the back of Windstorm's chair, "*Wise Ass,*" said a muffled voice. They knew it was Crawford and chuckled. He walked up behind the Pilots as they adjusted their standard flight settings and stood between them. He placed a hand on their shoulders. "*I'm going to put you both in for the Navigators Flying Cross and recommend a bonus, you both earned it.*"

Logan straightened his back and, in a respectful voice said, "*Thank you, Sir.*" Windstorm looked up at Crawford and, through a chuckle, said, "*Thank you First Officer.*" Crawford playfully flicked at Windstorm's left ear lobe, bent over, picked up the writing fob, and returned to his command chair. The Pilots looked at each other and gave a thumbs up.

Aden Representatives React

In the visitor's section the Aden Representatives screamed in terror as they watched the destruction of their home world, they went unconscious and collapsed to the floor. As the PDV flew to avoid the chunks of planet their bodies were thrown around. Crew Services crewmen in the section with the Adens had been injured as the large bodies slammed about.

During a moment of weightlessness, they managed to get away from the Adens. Advanced medical teams were not on the PDV, as no passengers were on board. Medics were called and responded to the visitor's section. The Chief Medic had other Medics apply emergency suspension bags.

The Adens stood forty feet tall, and the suspension bags began to wrap up their legs, moving toward their head. *"I will notify First officer this will hold them for two cycles. Enough phase to get them to Mars or Minertha, the Poor bastards."* said the Chief Medic.

Emergency Suspension bags are used on battlefields when the wounded or severely injured can't be bandaged or treated on sight. The bags formed around the humanoid body, augmented or non-augmented, as they are a gel and mercury mixed cellulose substance. After the injured party is encased in the substance, the metal cools, and the body would hibernate.

What have you done

Aden fractured in slow motion fashion. It appeared to expand and spread out as if a vibration from within the planet shook it apart. The large chunks of the planet spread out left and right, nothing went up or down, the large chunks formed a line or a belt within the same orbit the planet had taken for eons.

Lightning flashed between the chunks, which registered a magnetic field. Vessels in orbit outside the water membrane reversed course to avoid the large hunks of the planet and the water membrane that flew toward them. Fragments of the water membrane that were torn away from the planet trapped vessels in balls of water and immobilized them.

As they floated into space the water froze into solid ice, and the captive vessel was no longer visible. Most of the smaller vessels and cargo vessels that were lost could not accelerate faster than the debris or didn't have strong deflective shielding.

As the Scientists helped each other up they returned to their work stations. Others assisted those who were injured. Sufjan scanned the debris field for life forms, and found humanoid forms clumped together on a chunk of the planet, which still had atmosphere. He focused the scan on the group and noticed they were morphing into other creatures.

Puzzled at what he was seeing he analyzed the scan. The humanoid forms weren't human. As he magnified his view screen and tighten the scan beam the forms morph into many types of body shapes. Some shapes were unrecognizable animals or types of lifeforms he had never seen before.

Other scientists scanned the balls of water and the balls of ice. When a vessel was discovered inside the ice ball the scientist recorded the shape and density of the ball, this information could be used to locate the ball of ice by rescue vessels. Sufjan recorded the image of a humanoid form as it stood in a grassy area.

The atmosphere around the form was dissipating when it began morphing into different forms. The form now resembled a space worm with large claws and the legs grew together to form a fish tail and fin. As the creature grew the atmosphere was gone and the creature swam out into space.

He looked away from his view screen as he felt dizzy from the surreal image. He noticed other scientists were helping Gazou up and they sat him in a chair. He turned and continued to scan the chunks of planet. As he focused on the chunks that had flashed lightning, and recorded the energy output levels, the return data showed the debris field was highly magnetic.

After opening another tab on his computer, and inserting the data. A model of the chunks showed the magnetic power with a postulated data read out. He determined the magnetic pull could capture a rescue vessel and trap it on the surface. He bowed his head as the gravity of what has occurred pressed on his chest.

A feeling of sorrow welled inside him and teared his eyes. He thought *"There's nothing we can do. What a waste and for what?"* A voice called out, *"My readings are indicating all the bugs are dead, it worked. We're going to be rich."* Sufjan looked at Gazou and stormed toward him.

He spun the chair around, leaned forward, and placed his hands on the arms of the chair, and glared at Gazou. In a soft menacing voice he asked, *"What have you done? You have destroyed the planet and all of us along with it, ... you ... "*as he stood up and raised his hand to strike Gazou, a hand grabbed his wrist.

"Think about this," a voice said behind him. Sufjan kept glaring at Gazou, wanting more than ever to strike him. *"Think about this, we have created a new weapon and everything we did is separated into different files. We all own the intel property and process. We are going to be mega rich."* the voice said.

Sufjan tugged trying to strike Gazou. A hand grabbed his opposite shoulder and the voice said, *"Think about this JSO 10. We destroyed a moon. Nobody gives a jack crap about a moon. Don't forget all the people have been evacuated. JSO, think, eight thousand miles, think, a moon not a planet."*

Sufjan said, *"We made an illegal weapon and were deceptive about it, we'll be hung." "Maybe JSO, maybe, but that's why we have to leave now, we need off the PDV. We need to plan how and when we're going to jump ship. I am asking you to play your part until we leave."*

Sufjan relaxed and the hand came off his wrist. He turned around and looked at Water Resource Scientist Burbach, RSO12 and said, *"I'll play my part, because I'm not clean in this, Not, for him." "That's all I ask, and don't harm him, we need a sacrificial lamb if this gets, Sticky." "You can't be trusted, everyone knows that. I'm next in the command chain, you take My orders now."*

Clear all Channels

Smaller chunks of the planet that hurled toward PDV-109 were vaporized by the vessel's automated defensive measures or bounced off the massive vessel's deflective shields. Nottap said, "*Comms, contact the Wrath Group and have them rally at our plotted destination.*" "*Aye, Sir.*"

"*Nav, send the Wrath Group our plotted Course.*" Tracker stood up and turned around to face Nottap and Crawford as they sat in their command chairs. Crawford noticed him and nudged Nottaps' right arm, he pointed at Tracker, who was standing at attention to their left, and they both looked at him.

Tracker said, "*Sirs, the Olympus Wrath Landers Group was destroyed as the planet exploded, their transponders showed they had cleared the water membrane, and their vessels transmitted an impact signal that ended abruptly, no wreckage, no survivors.*"

Nottap looked at Tracker, gave no reply, and stared at him. Crawford said, "*Thank You, Nav Officer, please send all information concerning their mission to my PDT.*" "*Aye, Sir,*" replied Tracker as he sat down and swiveled his chair to face the navigation panel. Nottap gripped the arms of his command chair, he leaned forward and looked down at his feet as tears formed in his eyes.

He whispered, "*I did that, ... I did that... I did that...*" Crawford grabbed Nottaps right forearm with a firm grip, leaned over, and whispered, "*Stop it! The crew needs you to be strong now. We don't have phase for this. Make the announcement, order Comms to ring the Quarter bell ten tolls.*"

He let go of Nottaps forearm, sat upright in his Command chair, and adjusted his shirt. Nottap inhaled and exhaled as he wiped the tears from his cheeks and stood up.

He turned to look at Porter, and in a strong voice, said, *"Comms, clear all channels for an announcement. After the channels clear, call "Attention on deck." I will make the announcement, and signal you to sound the quarter bell ten tolls. After the tenth toll, I will call out the last port benediction. Are you clear?"*

Porter had been watching Nottap and Crawford, he too, had tears in his eyes. He nodded his head *yes*, swiveled his chair to face the comms panel, and transmitted over all channels with a shaky voice." *Clear all channels for an announcement, clear all channels."*

After all the channels fell silent, he turned on the vessel's PA system, which gave a boatswain whistle. He called out, *"All hands attention on deck. All hands attention on deck."* The bridge crew stood at attention, as did all the crewmen throughout the PDV. Porter turned toward Nottap and gave him a nod.

Nottap said in a clear voice, *"Attention, all hands, this is your Commander. This vessel has lost ten members of her crew. Hold fast for ten."* With that, Porter shouted, *"All hands, Salute."* All the crewmen on the bridge and throughout the PDV stood at attention and saluted.

Porter leaned over and turned on the quarter bell with a two-second delay per toll, it began to toll. After the tenth toll rang out, Porter turned and pushed a button on the comms panel. He turned toward Nottap and nodded.

Nottap said, *"All hands, the final port benediction, DILECTUS AMICUS GLORIOSUS, IN PERPETUUM, NAVIS RECTA ET VERA NAVIGANS. Our brothers, may the stars guide you home and make your course free and clear. Fair thee well."* Nottap gave Porter a nod.

Porter shouted, "*All hands, recover salute.*" Nottap called out, "*All hands, "Remember the Nahttrid," "Remember the Ten," all hands carry on,*" and with that, Porter turned off the PA system.

He sat down in his chair and, with a firm voice, transmitted, "*All channels are now clear for transmissions.*" Nottap sat in his Command chair and stared at the forward screen. Crawford walked around to each station and had whispered conversations with each crewman.

Nottap noticed a new message on his PDT, it was from his father. He stared at the name with a dazed look. A sense of shame came over him, and tears formed in his eyes. Crawford sat down, and Nottap lowered his PDT and wiped the tears from his eyes.

Crawford leaned toward Nottap and whispered, "*Shake it off, Sir, these things happen, and as a Commander, you need to be strong for your men. This is part of being in command. You good?*" "*I don't have a choice. I must be good for my men.*" "*Aye, Sir, you're good.*"

Mars Look Out!!

Crawford looked at Tracker, "*Nav, notify Mars Military and Civil Command the projectile is heading toward their planet, ETA to impact thirty five phases.* "*Aye, Sir.*" Tracker sent a message to MMC, "*PDV-109 Navigation Officer to Mars Military Command, I'm tracking the projectile and will transmit course and velocity data in real intervals.*"

MMC confirmed the transmission, and moments later, Tracker received a message from MMC, "*Mars Military Command to PDV-109 Navigation Officer, receiving data and need confirmation on the velocity numbers. The projectile should have slowed after impact with Aden not increased, MMC standing by.*"

Tracker looked at Nottap, "*Sir, Mars Military Command is requesting a confirmation on the velocity data.*" Nottap walked over to the navigation panel and connected. He sent a message that read, "*PDV-109 Commander to MMC the current velocity numbers are correct. The current course should have the projectile passing at a low altitude near the equator. Take all precautions to avoid this area, PDV-109 Commander Out.*"

Several vessels in orbit outside the Mars water membrane had focused cameras on the estimated area. Several vessels that flew under the water membrane near the estimated area also transmitted a live broadcast.

Tracker received a message from MMC, "*MMC to PDV-109 requesting specific data on projectile expected altitude, will the projectile pass miles above the surface, or should we duck? Please narrow your estimated altitude, MMC standing by.*"

Vessels in Orbit around Mars sent messages to Mars Air and Space Traffic Control (MASTC) to express their condolences to the citizens of Aden for the loss of their planet and loved ones.

They offered to relocate as many Adens as possible to their own home world if they desired. In response, the Martian Civilian Leadership sent a recorded message to all vessels in orbit: "*Thank You, from the people of Aden, we are currently waiting for a response from the Galactic Council for advisement of relocation and reparation. Again, Thank You.*"

MC Officers and MASTC Managers shook their heads in total disbelief that Martian Civilian Leadership was speaking for the people of Aden. The Martian Civilian Leadership had terminated the live video feed before the destruction of Aden. MC Officers concluded the Civilian Leaders were attempting to cover up the destruction of Aden and hide their censoring of the broadcast.

MASTC changed the recorded message, "*MASTC to all orbiting vessels, the projectile is heading for Mars, you're advised to maintain a safe distance and stand by to assist, MASTC out.*" As MC had declared Marshall Law, all Martian and Aden Civilians were ordered to secured bunkers in their cities or immediate areas. The Martian Civilian leadership was transferred from MC Headquarters to their secured bunker.

MC advised the Civilian Leadership they will not be allowed to give input on any and all future decisions. The citizens of Aden on Mars and Martian citizens had yet to be informed of Aden's destruction. The live broadcast was cut off due to the censorship by the Civilian Leadership.

MC sent a message to the Civilian leadership bunker, "*Military Command to Civilian Leadership. You must inform the citizens of the destruction of Aden, and the incoming projectile. Be advised the message from Leadership must explain the need for censorship, the grave threat of the projectile to our planet, and the need for their cooperation. Send your message for broadcast immediately. Military Command out.*"

Civilian Leadership sent a message to MC with a heavy party-political slant. MC responded with a message, "*This event is not, and will not, be a political issue, all levels of government are now inactive, Military Command out.*" The Aden and Mars Civilian Leadership had been viewing the Aden Military channel and witnessed the destruction of Aden.

Aden Civilian Leadership suffered the same terror as their counterparts on board PDV-109. The Martian Civilian leadership denied insinuations by MC, they had attempted to cover up or distort the truth of the event for political gain by the liberal Leadership.

The Truth of the Situation

After the secured bunkers personnel reported to MC the bunkers were full, near capacity, or had space available, MC rebroadcast the video of Aden's destruction to the civilian secured bunkers. Many Martians and Adens were confused and upset when MC declared Marshall Law and ordered everyone into the secured bunkers when the view screens went blank.

Military Command, believing that the rebroadcast of the live event would reveal *the truth of the situation*, aimed to unite all the people and gain their cooperation. The video, showing the impact projectile as it exited Aden on approach to Mars, was a stark reminder of the imminent danger. MC's belief was not unfounded. Reports flooded in from the civilian bunkers, recounting tales of civilians running out of the bunkers and pulling in those who were hesitant.

Once inside, the reluctant watched the videos, and the truth was laid bare. The civilians had banded together on a global scale, searching for anybody outside of a sturdy structure, demonstrating their unity and resilience in the face of adversity. The entire civilian population assisted each other in any way they could.

A well-known and trusted Martian journalist, Kannon Roland, conducted a live broadcast to assure the capital city's residents that the projectile would not strike the city. She reported that almost everyone was in a secured bunker and she and her crew would be heading to one soon.

She held up a small journal and claimed she picked up the journal that belonged to Liberal Party Member Daehtihs Archuleta, the Representative for the Northern Territory. Roland claimed Archuleta dropped the book out of his coat as he pushed his way to a transport, knocking over a woman and her children.

She read a short excerpt written by Daehtihs in his journal on the live broadcast, " *We hide the past, which leaves us free to control the future. The Planets Aden and Minertha must be hidden from the people.*

I propose a name change for Aden and Minertha. Aden switch vowel A for E to get Eden. Write a false narrative that includes a false location. Fund Archeologist to search for the Garden of Eden. Burn all records of the god Aden and destroy all statuary with his likeness. This will keep the masses "EYES DOWN" and not looking up for Planet Aden.

Fund religions that will erase the name "Aden" from all religious records and reprint all their Bibles or Doctrine letters at no cost to them. Use a smear campaign for those religions that will not comply, again EYES DOWN."

Minertha, drop "MIN" and move the vowel A behind E to get Earth, it becomes mythological. The vowel switch adds credibility to the "ancient name." Change the name of Goddess Minertha to Goddess Minerva. Write a false narrative and history for this Goddess. Make the claim the ancients misspelled her name frequently. Create forgery paintings and writings with misspelled titles to support the claim.

This will add to the credibility of the statement and misperception of the historical record of the Goddess. Portray the inhabitants of both planets as hostile alien invaders. Create and fund a civilian space program based on scientific research.

This program will be a private entity with no governmental connection or oversight, but it appears to be a branch of the government. The program will be funded by funneling funds budgeted for public education.

This space program will be overfunded and registered on the market place as a private entity, which will allow private groups to syphon funds without notice or accountability.

Under this program, air mines and detection devices will be reported as scientific data gathering. The real purpose is to detect and destroy vessels from "Minertha" or "Aden." Create a special Space Force branch of the military. We need a war that can't be seen or monitored, allowing all the Leaders to extort more resources from the people."

After reading the excerpt from the journal, Kannon Roland delivered a powerful commentary. *"Archuleta and his party,"* she declared, *"Can't be trusted to tell the truth, and should step down or be removed from Leadership positions permanently."*

This bold statement underscored the importance of truth and transparency in leadership, instilling a sense of justice and fairness in the audience. MC also rebroadcast Kannon Roland's news cast with the statement, *'The live broadcast of the destruction of Aden, was cut off due to the censorship by the Civilian leadership. Marshall Law will remain in effect until a proper military investigation, and or trial can be conducted. Now, is not the suitable phase, the projectile will be arriving soon.'*

Contingency Plan

The Grigorians on Mars and Minertha had been monitoring the events on Aden. Both contingents were small, with thirty members each. With the loss of their Command chain and all the others of their known population, with the destruction of Aden, they were a bit jumpy. They also realized, for now, they were on their own.

On Mars the Grigorians had shape-shifted into humanoid form and would maintain it until they felt safe. They formulated a plan to join the others on Minertha. Marshall Law had been declared on Mars, which meant intense scrutiny of individuals and freedom of movement would be restricted.

The Grigorians on Minertha planned to leave when the others arrived from Mars. They suspected that with all this activity, both planets would declare Marshall Law. The plan was to travel across the solar system and park in orbit around Neptune. Neither the Martian nor the Minerthan Military had TMS technology, and couldn't detect them.

A contingency plan was also discussed, as some Grigorians predicted the EF Troopers would arrive soon. The plan was basic: stay on Minertha and shape-shift into a herd or flock of animals or birds.

The Wise One, the leader of the Mars group, would be the leader for both groups as he was over ten thousand years old. He ordered the leader of the Minertha group, Isolep, to search for a secluded area with abundant animal life.

Isolep had her group search for a lush jungle region, as she preferred for them to morph back into their original forms, such as lizards, alligators, turtles, dragons, and chameleons. These forms also used less energy, which meant they would not need to eat often.

Nietsnief, squad one leader of the Minertha group, reminded Isolep they would need to maintain a body structure larger than the forty-foot humanoids. He suggested they morph into the Osaurs, a four-legged long-neck leaf eater found on their home world. Isolep agreed, and they began their search for a good location.

Isolep led the group north and reminded them she was eight thousand years old, and her old bones and joints needed sunshine and warmth. Oteb, a young egg stealer, reminded Isolep that the group would still need protein and suggested they find a feeding ground close to the leafy area.

Apocholis, a warrior, grabbed Oteb by his neck and threw him to the back of the group. Isolep looked at Apocholis and said in a hiss, *"These younger ones need to learn "Do Not Speak Unless Spoken To."* Apocholis replied with a hissed voice, *"Yes, Mistress."*

After traveling several miles through a forest, they came upon the edge. There before them, was a field of tall grass. Nietsnief looked at Apocholis and hissed, *"Check it out."* Apocholis looked at his squad and hissed, *"Brachi, you go north, Apat you go west and Camara you go east. I will take point. Don't bunch up we need to expand to our fullest."* The squad hissed in agreement.

Apocholis ran in to the field and expanded into a four-legged leafeater. The group were stunned as his height was eighty feet. Brachi looked at Apat, with wide eyes. They both ran into the field and expanded their bodies. Brachi stood seventy-five feet as did Apat. Camara charged into the field and expanded to one hundred ten feet.

As the others followed, they did the same. Oteb, could only expand to sixty-five feet. The heard of Osaurs kept traveling north, they could see trees with broad leaves not far away. Oteb expelled secretions and sent a message to the Wise One, *"Sir, we are a heard of thirty Osaurs and will send you coordinates for a landing zone."*

A Great Scar

The impact projectile pierced the water membrane at high velocity and passed through without resistance. It streaked across the Martian sky toward the planet, and the access doors and tail fins flew off. The high velocity kept the main body intact. Stage two maintained a solid connection with stage one. The projectile now appeared to be a robust cylinder. The water membrane wobbled and rippled like water in a lake after a rock was dropped.

The projectile slammed into the planet at an angle at the equator and gouged a path thousands of miles long and hundreds of miles wide. Other parts of the projectile flew off and also impacted the planet's surface, creating deep impressions in the shape of the object. The debris field was evidence of the velocity of the projectile.

While scraping along the surface, the payload canister ruptured, and a small stream of modified gamma radiation began to leak. Tremors from the impact area spread out, and a loud, vibrating sound was thrown into the water membrane. This caused the water membrane to vibrate in an unstable manner. The unstable water membrane began to thin, which caused snow to fall at higher altitudes.

As the tremors spread around the planet, many modestly built structures crumbled and fell. The debris from the gouged area was thrown in the same direction as the impact projectile as it dug across the surface. It began to gain altitude at the horizon curve of the planet, and flew off the surface at a high velocity, with rock debris trailing behind it.

As the ripples in the water membrane slowed, large waves formed. The projectile pierced the water membrane as it exited, which caused the water membrane to constrict and turn to ice.

It sprayed water into space from the entry and exit hole. A vessel in orbit outside the water membrane transmitted a live broadcast, wide-angle view of Mars as it sprayed water into space from two holes. One hole was in the east, and the other in the west. The transmitted images of Mars at the equator looked like a "*Great Scar*" on the surface.

Expedi Force Depart Saturn

As the Air Support vessel arrived at Saturn, the flotilla departed. Their orders from the Galactic Council had changed: Take the command and crew of PDV-109 into custody and take control of their vessel.

The Grigorians' prediction had come to pass. The Expedi Force had departed Saturn and was on its way to the inner solar system. With advanced technology on their vessels, they would be able to find the Grigorians and their vessels. They began to formulate a new plan. Regroup on Minertha and burrow into the mantel.

From prior battles, they knew GMF Troopers had TMS devices implanted in their helmet visor that could identify them in any form. This technology was effective within forty feet of an individual.

Through their collective consciousness, they knew GMF Expedi Force Troopers were well equipped and battle hardened, which made them a great threat. They didn't know the modified Expedi Force Troopers were on their first mission.

As the Grigorians on Mars returned to their scout vessel, which they left in a tropical zone, they discovered it was gone. They searched the immediate area and noticed footprints in the dirt. Exuctolis, a warrior, turned on the vessel locator, the return data showed it was in a salvage yard outside the Capital City.

They began to search for vessels to use as transport off Mars. More and more vessels were held for evacuation procedure by order of Military Command.

They had a plan: transform into Mars Troopers, obtain a Trooper transport vessel, and leave the base headed to MC Base Liberty. In between radar sweeps, they would alter course, pass through the water membrane, and go to Minertha.

Mars Troopers had modern weapons but lacked the TMS devices and couldn't detect the shape-shifted Grigorians. It was a risky plan, but the chaos would be a perfect distraction, it may work.

The Grigorians headed to a remote Trooper training base, which was used primarily for Airborne Vessel Assault and Ground Assault insertion Training. Two Grigorians' shapes shifted into Mars Command Officers, and they beguiled the training command staff into releasing an older vessel to them.

Flight Control for the training base was told the vessel would depart and fly to MC Base Liberty. There, they would stand by for further deployment. As two mechanics brought the ship from the hanger to the loading pad, the Grigorians, appearing as Officers and Troopers, climbed aboard.

Two Mechanics exited, and the vessel turned toward the take-off zone. After the vessel was airborne, the two pilots watched the radar sweep. After it passed their vessel, they turned on a red light in the cabin. Clicking was heard as the others fastened their seat belts. As the radar sweep passed their vessel again, they altered course and climbed toward the water membrane.

Mars Trooper Transport Vessels were not generally used for deep space or planetary travel. Older training vessels, however, had internal rather than external engines that could be modified while in flight. Travel would be slow until the modifications were complete.

Each Grigorian shape-shifted into a different humanoid form until they found the form that knew how to modify the internal engines. Nelle, a warrior, hissed, "*This one, this one knows how to do it.*" Nelle was now an augmented humanoid wearing an explorer group uniform. Several others shape-shifted into that form and worked together to modify the engines.

We are here for recruits

Military Command had released the civilian populace from the secured bunkers with an "*all clear*" signal. Many environmental scientists had observed the water membrane for stability and noticed that the ripples had changed to tsunami waves that raced across the sky. The air had become thin, and the humidity had dropped noticeably.

Citizen weather watchers called local atmospheric stations to report their observations. They observed balls of ice that fell from the water membrane as the tsunami waves passed overhead. Many angry Aden and Martian citizens waited outside the secured bunkers of the civilian leadership, as they had not yet emerged.

Several men attempted to pry open the doors, however, the doors were locked from the inside. Troopers arrived in vehicles, and a Captain asked the large crowd to gather around for several announcements. As the Captain was about to speak, he noticed a tsunami wave on the horizon's edge, moving fast.

He informed the citizens that balls of ice would fall from the wave and to take shelter immediately. The captain and his men took shelter in a civic building, while throngs of citizens took shelter in nearby shops and any structure that appeared to be solid.

A few of the Aden civilians refused to take shelter, as they assumed this was an attempt by the military to remove the civilian leadership from the bunker to protect them.

Ice balls slammed down with great force and Aden citizens covered their heads, but their forty-feet bodies were pummeled by the eight-feet ice balls. Several were killed, others were severely injured. As the storm moved on, the Captain and Troopers exited the building, and he called an all-clear.

As he walked back to his vehicle, he called for the citizens to come back out into the open. As the citizens trickled back, he addressed the remaining crowd and asked former Troopers to report to the nearest military base to lend a hand however possible.

A Trooper nudged the captain, and whispered in his ear. The captain cleared his throat and said, *"Also, any able-bodied man or woman who could pilot a space vessel register with ASTC should the evacuation of our planet become necessary."*

Shouts rang out, *"What about those cowards hiding in their hole? We want them out here, now!"* He looked behind him at the shelter doors, turned, faced the crowd, and gestured for quiet. He shouted, *"We are not here for them. We are here to find recruits. Get the injured to medic stations and clear those bodies from the streets, carry on."*

The Captain and Troopers climbed into their vehicles and drove away. The crowd closed in on the doors and began to bang on them with hammers and other objects.

What is a flooded area

Environmental scientists across Mars urgently studied information sent in concerning the tsunami waves. These waves had combined into one colossal wave, and the ice balls that once fell had ceased, replaced by a relentless downpour of rain as the tsunami wave passed overhead.

Information from vessels orbiting outside the water membrane revealed a constant rate of water loss, leading the scientists to calculate that the Mars water membrane would be depleted in a mere two hundred years.

Effects of the two holes were already being felt at higher altitudes. Air was thinner, and the temperature had dropped. Ice balls from the tsunami wave that didn't melt rolled down mountainsides. Plants of all kinds withered and died, trees lost their leaves and stood bare. Water was collected in lower areas, which formed lakes that swelled and flooded.

Rivers were formed and dangerous to cross. Environmental Scientists attempted to forecast which areas would be in danger of flooding but had no information to evaluate the situation.

Heavy rain had washed out many of the direct lines of communications, or hampered radio communications. Martians in remote areas, despite taking shelter in underground bunkers, found themselves trapped as the bunkers flooded. The water was too heavy to allow the doors to open outward, leaving them in a state of helplessness.

More and more communities were cut off from any line of communication, and those who were above ground struggled to make their way to cities, some being swept away by fast undertow currents. MC ordered air attack vessels to circle the outer areas of the cities to get an aerial view of the flooded areas.

Ground Troopers were ordered to report to the flooded areas to assist citizens. Pilots and ground crewmen reported to MC that the air attack vessels wouldn't start due to the high moisture. The air attack vessels flew using natural static discharge from the planet, which was no longer present. Platoon leaders asked each other, "*What is a flooded area?*"

Mars had never experienced such an event, and Command Officers had no training for such a disaster. As more information came in, Commanders refused to send their ground Troops to the flooded areas, as most Martians had no reason to learn how to swim.

Look out Minertha

Aboard PDV-109, Porter received an encrypted message from Gov of Nav Corp. The message was titled "*PDV-109 Commander Priority One.*" Porter looked at Nottap, "*Sir, you have a priority one message from the Governance.*" Nottap walked over to his Command Chair, sat down, and picked up his PDT, he opened the message.

"*Governance of the Navigators Corporation and members of the Galactic council order the Planetary Developers Vessel-109 to end all operations immediately and hold the vessel on station. You are not to move the vessel to any port or transmit data to any entity. EF Troopers are on the way to take control of the vessel and place all personnel in custody pending a full review. Standing by for acknowledgment.*"

Nottap stood up and shouted, "*All eyes here.*" Crawford and the entire bridge crew stopped what they were doing and looked at Nottap. "*I received a message from Gov of Nav Corp.*" He read the message to his bridge crew. "*Do not acknowledge that message! DO NOT!*" shouted Crawford.

A loud, booming voice piped in over the speakers. "*It's headed to Minertha*!" shouted Dodson, the Launcher Tech who had monitored the bridge as he waited for orders.

Tracker sent a message to Minertha Air and Space Traffic Control (MNASTC): *PDV-109 Navigation Officer to MNASTC, the projectile is headed toward your planet. Transmitting flight path and velocity data in real interval PDV-109 out.*

With the impact on Mars, the projectile was severely disfigured and resembled more of a distorted metal pipe as it spun in an upright circular fashion end over end.

Sensor scans revealed modified gamma radiation was leaking, and vessels in the area were able to match the velocity. At the current velocity, the impact with Minertha was estimated to be four hours. PDV-109 Scientists attempted to compute the rate of gamma radiation depletion based on the readings from Mars, and the amount of gamma radiation that leaked out while in flight to Minertha.

Nottap called out, "*Status report, all stations.*" As they have been trained to give the status report verbally to the Officer on deck (OD), the pilots are the first to reply, followed by Navigation, Science, Engineering, Crew Services, Security, and Communications.

Logan said, "*Sir, cleared Mars, our eta is 0.015 phases to the plotted final destination. Vessel flight performance evaluation is complete and I listed it as successful in my report, Sir.*"

Tracker said, "*Sir, we are on the correct course, and I'm monitoring the projectile, it's heading and velocity, and sending data to Minertha Leadership and their Military Command, Sir.*"

Science Officer Wood said, "*Sir, computing...*" Porter cut him off, "*Commander, is that allowed, or advisable, considering the currently pending message from...*" he was cut off by Crawford, who, in a loud and commanding voice, shouted, "*Operations as usual, nothing changes, we are professionals and will act accordingly,*" the bridge crew responded with "*Aye, Sir.*"

Nottap looked at Porter, and in a calm voice said, "*What is happening on Mars? Are they going to evacuate?*"

"*No word, Sir,*" replied Porter in a subdued voice. Nottap replied, "*Aye, if they start to evacuate notify me immediately.*" "*Aye, Sir.*" Crawford called out "*Science, continue.*" "*Aye Sir, computing rate of gamma radiation depletion from the projectile. It will have a trace amount when it enters the Minertha water membrane, Sir.*"

After Wood gave his report there was a pause. Crawford stood up and looked at the engineering panel. No crewman was assigned to monitor Engineering, Crew Services, and Security as there were no passengers on board.

Crawford said, *"Comms, status report."* *"Aye, communications traffic has increased from vessels in the area. They're outside of the Copernican solar system. At last count four systems are sending vessels to Mars and Minertha. Their scout vessels are already here and have been monitoring our activities. They're sending reports back to their home worlds, the debris from Aden has a high metal and mineral count."*

He swiveled his chair and looked at Crawford, he didn't make eye contact and said in a subdued voice, *"GCR's are throwing a party on Saturn, and it sounds like it has to do with us. They mention the video from our probe and seventh branch of the Galactic Military after obtaining the data from PDV-109 Neiubo. That's all Sir."* Porter swiveled his chair and looked at his panel.

Crawford sat down and looked at his PDT, he leaned toward Nottap and asked, *"This is odd Sir, how could they have viewed our link to the probe? I told Comms, to make it a tight beam, quite odd."* *"Aye, First Officer, odd, what a mystery it is. Well, stay on task."* *"Aye, Sir."*

Full Blown Fubar

Crawford stood up and walked over to the communication panel. A voice over the speakers said, "*Commander, I'm feeling kind of sick from the rough ride. Can I go off rotation?*" It was Launcher Tech Dodson who monitored the bridge as he waited for orders. Nottap looked across the bridge at Crawford.

Crawford covered his mouth with his fingers and bowed his head. Nottap replied, "*Aye, you can go off shift, and thank you for your dedication to service.*" "*Aye, thank you, Sir, Launcher Control Out,*" replied Dodson, a click was heard when he turned off the intercom.

Nottap crossed his arms, and slowly walked over to Crawford where he stood next to the communication panel. "*Snafu?*" asked Nottap. "*Negative Sir, we are in full blown fubar,*" responded Crawford. Porter, Science Officer Wood and Crawford laughed.

Nottap looked at Crawford and asked, "*You're going to tell me what that means, right?*" Crawford replied, "*Aye, Sir.*" He shook his head and sighed as he turned and walked to his Command chair, he stopped spun around and looked at Crawford. "*Sir?*" asked Crawford. "*I get it. Three men walked into a bar. I get it.*" Crawford chuckled, "*Aye, Sir.*"

Nottap turned around and walked to his command chair. Crawford knelt down next to Porter, "*I wasn't yelling at you, I wasn't angry, we all need to be on the same page, okay?*" Porter, reached out his hand and the two shook hands.

Projectile Safe Guards

In the launcher section, Projectile Specialists and Launcher crewmen reviewed the event data. The probe, which gave the first report of the projectile as it exited Aden, reported that the projectile's velocity had increased when it should have slowed.

Standard safeguards on the Impact Projectile itself didn't initiate an immediate self-destruct, which was a great concern for both departments. Without the standard safeguards in place, the explosive head could have detonated at any step of the process.

The impact Projectile's safe guards after launch are: "*Any deviation of the flight path more than 25 feet, loss of signal from the launch vehicle, sudden impact with any solid object during flight to the impact area.*"

As the launcher crewmen reviewed their data, regular documentation was missing from the database. With the help of a Projectile Specialist, they searched the Science and Engineering database, they kept getting the message, "*No Record Found.*"

The probe passed through the water membrane with no problem. Science Manager Gazou expected the impact projectile's second stage to do the same despite the obvious differences in build and size.

As the projectile spun toward Minertha, its velocity decreased, however, the rate of spin increased. The shape of the spinning object narrowed from a wobble to an inline spin.

The debris that trailed behind appeared to be "*Acting Oddly,*" which gave the projectile a hurricane-on-edge appearance.

Projectile Specialist Crew Chief Costello asked Launcher Crew Chief Abbott for the exact procedure for prepping and loading, particularly if the projectile had been bumped or dented.

Chief Abbott asked Chief Costello for the build schematics used to construct the Impact Projectile. Costello replied, "*We didn't build it. We modified an 18-gram impact projectile second stage and explosive head, using the schematics provided by the Scientists.*" When Abbott was given the schematics, he gruffly said, "*It was a perfect load, no bumping or denting. It's only 8 grams, for goodness' sake. Even you could load that up.*"

At a glance, Abbott noticed the schematics were in seven different files. He asked Costello, "*Why are the schematics split up and not in one file?*" "*Aye, like I said, we modified an 18-gram impact projectile second stage and explosive head for the Scientists. They split the file. Why they did that, I don't know.*"

Abbott noticed four power systems and all safety protocol systems were not listed, most notably the detonation device, which triggers immediate self-destruction. The components necessary to separate the first stage from the second stage had the power source listed as "*Remove.*"

All the standard safeguards for the explosive head had "*Remove*" with a note: "*Add Thymol Glycerin.*" Abbott put his right finger-knuckle in his mouth and bit down to muffle a scream. Costello looked at him and asked, "*What? What do you see?*" He took the PDT from Abbott, looked at it momentarily, and shouted, "*Oh mighty Rah!*"

"*What were they thinking? We are so screwed. Thymol Glycerin?*" Costello checked the cover sheet and noticed the only signature of approval was from Gazou. The Science Department Crew Chiefs had initialed the line by their name. Costello said, "*I need to sit down,*" and flopped into a chair.

As he read on, he noticed the gravity weight was not changed on the schematic. During launch preparation, the Impact Projectile's gravity weight was listed as two-thirds less. He handed the PDT to Abbott and asked, "*What size propellant was used for this launch?*"

Abbott walked over to Launcher Propellant Tech Hazel and, in a whispered voice, asked, "*How much propellant did you use on this launch?*" Tech Hazel whispered, "*The required amount for this weight is smaller than what we have, so I used one of the smallest pellets in inventory, 18 grams, Only ONE Chief.*"

Abbott looked at him, puzzled. "*You knew the projectile's weight was under 18 grams, and you used the propellant anyway? Why didn't you say anything?*" "*I did. I told the Science Manager, and he yelled, 'Launch it!'*" Abbott nodded his head and, in a whispered voice, said, "*Keep that between us for now, it may save our behinds.*" Hazel looked at him bewildered and whispered, "*Sure thing, Chief.*"

While looking at the schematics, Abbott yelled out, "*As far as this goes,*" as he pointed at the schematics. "*Projectile Specialists and Launcher Crewmen will be sent to internment camps or salvage labor planets after a short trial. As this is proof, we all built and launched an illegal weapon.*"

What's this we stuff

"What's this, WE, stuff?" called out a Launcher crewman. With that, other Launcher crewmen began to argue with the Projectile Specialists. Their voices grew louder as each side refused to accept fault for their actions and called the other side deceptive. The exchange was intense and pointed.

Projectile Specialists accused the launcher crew of mishandling the projectile and improper load procedure. The launcher crew accused the Projectile Specialists of modifying the projectile without authorization from command, outside of protocol, and not updating the launch data report.

Both Crew Chiefs did their best to keep the conversation on track and prevent it from becoming physical. It became obvious to Abbott that the powder keg of highly emotional men was at the explosion point when he jumped onto a work table and yelled, *"ENOUGH, STOP, EVERYONE, STOP."*

The group of angry men stopped and looked at him. *"We must all hang together, or we will all be hung separately, I assure you."* He said confidently, *"We all were set up to take the fall, but together, we can expose the truth, but not if we fight each other. I have a plan."*

A Projectile Specialist asked Abbott, *"How do you know there will be an investigation or a trial?"* Abbott replied, *"Don't be daft. Do you think we can blow up a planet, and nobody inquire about it? They are probably already sending people our way along with GMF Troopers, who will not be the friendliest."*

Launcher Tech Dodson said, *"Aye, He's right, they are. I monitored the bridge, waiting for orders from the First Officer when the Commander read a priority one message from the Gov of Nav Corp and the Galactic Council. Troopers will take us all into custody."*

They had to say that

As PDV-109 passed Mars, Tracker noticed a Mars military vessel exiting the water membrane. "*Sirs, a Mars Military vessel exited the water membrane and fell in line behind us.*" Crawford stood up and walked over to the navigation panel. He sat in the second seat and scanned the vessel.

It was an older Olympus Wrath Landing Vessel, a second-generation model. He tapped Tracker's left arm, pointed at the screen, and chuckled, "*I think our Elder Fathers would remember this model.*"

Tracker looked at the vessel description and said, "*That's a classic. Amazing, it's still spaceworthy. How many missions do you think that old war horse has seen?*" Crawford sent the data to his PDT, saying, "*They are brave souls. It's a Trooper transport configuration with a full load. They could be going to Minertha to assist, or they may have evacuees on board.*"

He looked at Tracker and said, "*Put a travel marker on it for now, and let us know if it starts to close on us.*" "*Aye, Sir.*" Crawford walked over to the communications panel, "*Comms, we have a Mars military vessel behind us, it could be looking to board us or going the same direction to Minertha, we don't know. Don't hail or respond to their hail. Record any messages they transmit or receive. If they are given orders to board us sound general quarters. Are we good?*"

"*Aye, First Officer and we're more than good Sir, we're brothers on the same page.*" Crawford patted Porter's shoulder. "*Aye, we are.*" Crawford returned to his Command chair and sat down. He looked at his PDT and noticed he had received a message. Nottap looked at Crawford, shook his head, and, in a sarcastic voice, rhetorically asked, "*What could go wrong? What could go wrong?*"

He sighed and said in a chuckle, "*They had to say that?*" Crawford looked at him with a grin, "*Our fate is our own, you are still in Command, Sir.*"

Nottap smiled and nodded briskly, "*Thank you, First Officer. I am still in Command.*" "*Sir, have you thought about how you will respond to the message?*" "*Aye, First Officer, but for now I'm not going to respond. After I think about our options, I will tell you how I will respond.*"

"*Aye, Sir. I'm going to assist Nav with tracking incoming military vessels. I think we will be getting busy soon.*"Nottap gave a nod, "*Aye, carry on.*"

Opportunists

Crawford took the secondary screen position at the navigation panel and scanned for military vessels only. He would occasionally turn to look over the bridge, he felt if the crew could see him, this would keep them from becoming "*nervous.*"

Tracker looked at Crawford and said, "*Sir, there are three flotillas headed our way. Well, I mean toward the Copernican solar system, and their vessel identifiers do not match up with their nav markers.*" "*Aye, move them to my screen. I will take a look.*" "*Aye, Sir, they should be on your screen now, Sir.*" "*Aye, Nav, I have them.*"

Crawford focuses on the flagships for each flotilla. His screen showed the first flagship vessel identifier as "*Aztecs Tiotiagohucan TAURUS, Mesos Elnath,*" the second flagship vessel identifier as "*Ullor Marono PLEIADES Amalienborg,*" and the third showed "*Caspid canine CANCER Canis minor.*" He looked at Tracker and asked, "*Do these ID names mean anything to you?*"

Tracker looked at the names and sighed, "*Aye, Sir, those three planet groups are known for privateers or opportunists, scavengers by trade. They can be friendly if the trade is good, but that can change instantly.*"

Crawford looked at the screen and asked, "*What would happen if we got them to fight it out among themselves, winner-take-all? Who would win?*" Tracker laughed and said, "*Let's find out, Sir. Can you arrange that?*" "*Aye Nav, I know their mind. First, they must be going to pick through what's left of Aden. Second, all the flagships are stolen, guaranteed.*" They both laughed.

Crawford looked at the first flagship and asked, "*Nav, the flagship Aztecs Tiotiagohucan TAURUS, Mesos Elnath, what do you have on them.*"

"Aye, Sir, Aztecs, that's an acronym for their occupation, Astro Zinc Technicians, Az when communicating. They mine and make parts with Zinc. Tiotiagohucan, the name of their vessel, Tio Tiago Human, and Mesos Elnath, their city of origin and planet ... I show Mesos, Middle City, which is on planet Elnath, in the TAURUS planet cluster."

"Okay, Nav, do they get along with the other two?" "Well, Sir, it's hard to say, all three are listed as stolen vessels, and as I said, the vessel identifiers don't match their nav markers." "Aye, Nav, watch this. Comms, contact planet Elnath in the TAURUS system Mesos city and ask what the bounty is for their stolen vessel, the "Aztecs Tiotiagohucan." Send that on the general channel. "Aye, Sir."

Tracker and Crawford watch the navigational scope for several moments. They laughed when the TAURUS flotilla made an abrupt course change. Crawford said, "There goes the rabbit, let's hope those hounds give chase." "Aye, Sir, what if they ... Oh ...there they go ... "Tracker laughed as the flagship Caspid canine changed course, followed by its flotilla.

Crawford looked at Tracker and said, "That will keep them busy until there is a victor or an alliance. Comms, if we get a hail from the Ullor Marono, handle the call." "Aye, Sir." Tracker called out, "Comms, their nav marker is Polar Star." "Aye."

Nottap looked at Porter and said, "Comms, if you hear back from Elnath, let me know." "Aye, Sir." Nottap looked at Crawford and said, "You never know it might be a good side job." They all shared a hearty laugh.

Martians are being "Martians"

On Minertha, the leadership of the largest territory, Arkoma, contemplated the daunting task of declaring Marshall Law. With no one-world government or army, they knew they would need over two-thirds of the territories' votes, a near-impossible feat as the territories could not be forced to comply.

Due to its size, robust military, and thriving economy, Arkoma, the largest territory, held significant sway over planet-wide discussions. Its decisions often set the tone for the rest of the territories.

Each territory had its own governmental body and army. The registered citizens in a territory would vote on their issues. They couldn't force other territories to comply with their rules or regulations.

Arkoma leadership decided to advise all the territories' leadership of the situation and advised them to prepare their residents to enter a secured shelter if the need arose. Arkoma Military Command and Civilian leadership contacted Mars Military Command. They requested information on how their populace responded when Marshall Law was declared.

Mars Military Command replied, "*Prior to the declaration of Marshall Law, we advise you confine all Civilian Leadership to a secured bunker, have all Troops standing by, and inform all citizens of the "TRUTH of the situation."Citizens on Mars banded together to assist each other without pause once they were told the TRUTH about Aden.*"

On Minertha, all residents watched in horror as Aden was destroyed and the Mars water membrane pierced. There was no censorship, and the live broadcast wasn't interrupted in any way. Many Adens who were temporarily relocated to Minertha needed to be cared for medically and emotionally.

The response from MMC confused the Civilian Leadership, and they began to wonder if something else had happened and not a cosmic disaster.

A Civilian Leader for the Lailah Territory asked a Military Commander, "*Can you help me make sense of all this? Are we under attack? Are we at war?*" The Military Commander said, "*No, Advisor, we are not under attack or at war. The Martians are being, well, "Martians. Our intel shows they censored the Aden disaster, and our data and live broadcast show we will not need to declare Marshall Law.*"

The Civilian Leader let out a sigh, "*Thank you for letting me know. The Martians sure are a different group of people, I'll tell you that. It's always, "prepare for war, we're at war, blast that, blast this" crazy I say.*"

The Military Commander chuckled and said, "*Well, yes, I agree. They are a different group. You know their planet is named after the God of War. Have you noticed that if you turn the M in Mars upside down you get Wars. That could explain a lot.*"

Projectile Arrives

A vessel named Etum from the star system Rigel had established orbit outside the Minertha water membrane. The captain reported on the approach of the projectile to MNASTC. He offered to transmit a live broadcast of the projectile as it approached Minertha. MNASTC accepted the offer and sent a worldwide alert. *World Wide Alert Message: All Citizens, please connect to the following live broadcast for important information. The vessel Etum will be broadcasting a live view of the approaching projectile."*

Many people on Minertha connected to the live broadcast for information on the approaching projectile. They watched the screens as the vessel camera operator struggled to focus on the projectile. As the live broadcast began, the object looked like a gigantic hurricane on edge as it spun toward them.

"There it is Minertha, that's headed your way," said a voice from the screen. Many on Minertha froze as they looked at the massive object on the screen. Some residents felt as if their hearts had stopped others stopped breathing. The image of a gigantic hurricane swirling on edge, smashing large pieces of the planet together, was dark and blurry.

At first glance, it appeared Mars had been consumed and not grazed. A voice from the screen said, *"Oh, sorry about that. The lens setting is set to one hundred magnifications, I will reset it now, sorry."* As the residents watched the image, it shrank from a gigantic hurricane to the size of a ten-mile disk. The large hunks of planet smashing together were dirt clumps.

As the clumps broke apart it turned into a powder giving the dark hurricane hue around the pipe as it spun upright. A collective planet wide sigh of relief could be felt.

Leaving a splatter crack

As they all began to breathe again, many laughed, some laughed and cried as fear left their body, and some fell to their knees in great relief. The projectile began to slice into the water membrane. The water membrane constricted, and the projectile was shot out toward the planet. The projectile's second stage disconnected from the first stage, and the second stage engines ignited.

The first stage spun straight down and slammed into the ground, creating an impact crater. The second stage hit the ground at an angle, creating a large trench and digging deep into the mantle. A vessel under the water membrane began a live broadcast and gave the narrative the projectile looked like a splinter in the palm of your hand.

An air attack craft flew an oval pattern around the trench, transmitting images and data back to Military Command. The projectile detonated and destroyed air vessels in the area. The detonation created a large canyon in the mantel, which was hundreds of miles long, miles wide, and one mile deep.

The debris from the explosion was thrown up into the water membrane. A five-hundred-mile radius shock wave emanated from the explosion with such force, mountain tops were lifted off their foundations and slid into valley areas. Trees popped up into the air as if pushed from below.

Vessels entering the area relayed images of the site with the narrative, "*The fracture looks like a rock that had bounced off a pane of glass, leaving a splatter crack.*" As the water membrane shed off the debris in the form of heavy rain, the water fell into many low-lying areas and began to flood, creating lakes.

Civilian Leadership and Military Command had no plans for this event. Like Mars, it had never flooded on Minertha before.

The Greeks recorded this event as the first diluvium event on Minertha. However, the entire water membrane was not lost. One-third was now on land, and two-thirds were still in the sky.

This had an effect on the planet in the form of less oxygen and cooler temperatures, which equated to everything new growing smaller and with a shorter life span.

The Tartareans

On PDV-109, the Projectile Specialists and Launcher Crewmen had determined Science Manager Gazou ordered the design of the Impact Projectile and didn't inform Nottap or Crawford. The Modification of the 18-gram Impact Projectile was compartmentalized for secrecy. Gazou or Sufjan spoke to several Projectile Specialists "*Privately.*" After inflating the ego of the Projectile Specialist or the possibility of a share of "*The big bonus,*" the specialist would sign a nondisclosure agreement.

As the Projectile Specialists reported to the Science Department on their off-rotation, a Scientist gave each of them a schematic and had them perform a task on the 18-gram impact projectile. Gazou kept information from Nottap, all the Managers, the Launcher Crew, and Engineering Fabrication.

He put forward the narrative, "*ALL CALCULATIONS HAVE BEEN MADE!*" The scientists parroted his narrative. The revelation that Gazou would use the two units to bear the majority of fault if any unexpected adverse event occurred congealed the two units into one.

As one unit, the group decided to depart the PDV aboard Olympus Wrath Landing vessels and set course for Minertha. Waiting on Minertha was far more desirable than being held in custody by EF Troopers and sent to a detainment center to wait for the investigation and trial to conclude.

PDV-109 had many transport vessels to choose from. The Launcher Crew were all former GMF Troopers familiar with the Olympus.

GMF Troopers used the Olympus Wrath Landing vessels primarily for aerial recon, ground recon Trooper insertion, and silent assault deployment missions as it had "*cloaking ability*" technology.

Several Launcher crewmen were pilots during their tenure for GMF and maintained flight ratings for this vessel. Once the Olympus Wrath Lander was safely tucked away in orbit around Minertha, Abbott would transmit all the data and a video of each crewman reading their statement aloud.

In their individual video, each crewman would give an account of their activities or observations and avoid speculation or conjecture. Abbott advised them not to admit or confess to any wrongdoing and to emphasize that Science Manager Gazou approved this activity.

The completed file would only be transmitted to GMF Command and the Galactic Council. The crew felt no loyalty toward the Gov of Nav Corp. The new unit called themselves the Tartareans, as their uniforms were manufactured by the R. D. Tartar Uniform and Industrial PPE Equipment Corporation on Neiubo.

Chief, what could go wrong?

Turner, a Projectile Specialist, devised a distraction for this operation. Turner would use a rocket engine from a probe in the engine testing area. With the engine properly placed and secured in a test frame, all would look normal. The parameters entered into the computer for the test would also appear normal. He would use a timer on the ignition plug to ignite the engine.

The timer would melt away after the engine burned at full power. With the blast doors blocked open, this would set off the fire alarms in the area, making it appear to be a fire. Abbott was a bit nervous about the plan. Turner said, "*Chief, the fire suppression system will go off thirty seconds after the alarm. We all run down to the space dock, load, and go, so relax, Chief. What could go wrong?*"

Abbott gathered all the Launcher crewmen in an empty vessel hanger by the space dock. As the crewmen walked in, they talked to each other, and the common din of conversations filled the air. Abbott stood on a platform to count the crewmen coming in. As the last few arrived, he stepped off the platform and shouted, "*Attention on deck.*"

The crewmen stood at attention, facing Abbott. He called out, "*I'm going to give it to you in a nutshell. The last launch was as good as it gets. However, as you all may know by now, errors occurred, which put all launcher crewmen at risk of detainment, a short trial, confinement, or worse, sentenced to a salvage-yard labor planet. The Science Department Manager and the scientists set up the crew for failure from the jump. At ease and have a seat.*"

The crewmen sat down on cargo boxes in the immediate area of Abbott. A crewman said, "*Chief, how do you know they will put us in detainment? What proof do you have?*" asked a crewman.

Abbott said, "*A Launcher Tech overheard the Commander reading a priority one message from the Gov of Nav Corp advising him to stand by to be boarded. However, the Tech also heard the First Officer yell out, "Do not acknowledge the message." Fortune has smiled on us, as the First Officer is the brains of this vessel, but he can't save us if we are boarded. I wager the Commander will acknowledge the message.*"

Abbott picked up his PDT and held it high for all to see, "*This has the files from the Projectile Specialists who modified an 18-gram impact projectile. They made an illegal weapon without understanding what the end result would be. They followed the direction of the science manager, who held information from them. Each modification appeared to be inert, with the assumption that another Projectile Specialist would complete the next step. The projectile was handed off to the launcher crew. The launcher crew assumed it was a completed projectile, as any one of us would assume the same.*"

Abbott held up a second PDT and said, "*This has the launch data, which is incomplete and inaccurate. When the Science Manager was questioned about the missing or inaccurate data, he yelled "Launch the projectile." This launch was supervised and authorized by the Science Department Manager ONLY. Under current regulations, the launcher crew had to launch the projectile.*

We all know who will get thrown under the rubbish truck. We all know who was left holding the smoking gun, and we all know who will get the hangman's noose." A crewman from the back of the group yelled out, "*Not my problem. That's their problem, not ours. We did nothing wrong. I was off rotation, which, again, is not my problem.*"

Abbott said in a loud voice, "*Remember the Nahttrid? Eighty Launcher crewmen were detained for twelve cycles while Investigators searched for the guilty.*

They were held during an investigation of wrongdoing by two IT Techs. All eighty were released after their commitment to serve contract ended, while they were in detainment waiting for the investigation to end.

They didn't do anything wrong but were treated as guilty men. It is your problem. It is all our problem. They are coming to take us all. They won't search for the guilty, and that's not their job. The Investigators search for the guilty and always start at the top, with command, and work their way down to the bottom. Do you think the Science Manager will come clean? I don't."

The group looked at each other and murmured, some nodded their heads. "*What's your plan, Chief?*" shouted out a crewman. Abbott replied, "*We are throwing in with the Projectile Specialists. The Scientists tricked them into taking a fall, like the Launcher crew. We will depart the PDV aboard Olympus Wrath Landers and head to Minertha.*

Bring your personal items. If you can pack it, bring it. You will get the sign when we run down to the space dock, load, and go. If you're late, you're on your own. And remember, "Idle chatter, vessels splatter, the walls are always listening. Any questions?"

"*Aye, Chief, what if they accuse us of desertion?*" "*You all have to make the choice for yourself: go or stay. That's the plan, so be there or find a place to hide, as for us, we are leaving. Attention on deck, dismissed.*"

Final Destination

Logan said, "*Commander, we have arrived at the final destination coordinates.*" "*Aye, Pilot standard station keeping, maintain position.*" Nottap sat in his Command Chair, leaned forward, and looked down at his feet. He pounded the arms of his command chair with the palms of his hands and stood up. The air on the bridge became tense, and all eyes were on him.

He turned toward Porter, "*Comms, clear all channels for an announcement.*" Porter transmitted," *Clear all channels for an announcement, clear all channels.*" After the channels fell silent, he turned on the vessel's PA system, which gave a boatswain's whistle. He turned toward Nottap and gave him a nod.

Nottap spoke in a strong, loud voice, "*Attention, all hands, this is your Commander. I have received a message from the Gov of Nav Corp, it reads as follows: Governance of the Navigators Corporation and members of the Galactic council order the Planetary Developers Vessel-109 to end all operations immediately and hold the vessel on station. You are not to move the vessel to any port or transmit any data to any entity. EF Troopers are on the way to take control of the vessel and place all personnel in custody pending a full review, standing by for acknowledgment.*"

Nottap hesitated and looked at Crawford, who was across the bridge where he sat by the navigation panel. Crawford stood up and saluted. He gave Crawford a return salute and said, "*All crewmen in engineering shut down main engines and close all fuel valves, maintain life support and station-keeping thrusters. Report to the main auditorium for a briefing. All other crewmen secure your stations and report to the main auditorium, Commander Out.*"

With that, Porter turned off the PA system. Nottap fell back into his Command chair and covered his face with his hands as he leaned back and screamed. All eyes on the bridge were still on him.

He screamed again through his hands as he leaned forward and yelled, "*Could it get any worse?*" As some bridge crewmen moved forward to console him, Crawford made a silent motion to them. He waved his hand in the air to indicate, "*No.*" the bridge crewmen retreated to their positions.

Crawford said in a commanding voice, "*You're still in Command, Sir. What are your orders, Sir.*" With that, Nottap jumped up from his command chair angerly and stood up. With anger on his face, he wiped tears from his cheeks, adjusted his shirt, and stated with a firm commanding angry voice, "*This bridge is still active until further notice from ME, maintain all operations at your stations, we are in standard station keeping.*" The bridge crew responded with a loud and brisk, "*Aye, Sir.*"

Nottap took a deep breath and exhaled, "*Thank you, First Officer, I am still in Command*" he turned to face Tracker, "*What is the position of the Mars Trooper vessel?*" "*Sir, they stopped when we stopped, Sir,*" called out Tracker. Nottap looked at Porter and said, "*Comms, if Gov of Nav Corp send another priority one message, send it to my PDT, and do not respond.*" "*Aye Sir.*"

"*Comms, if they want other information, reply with, sorry, we are busy saving lives. Short and sweet, GOT IT?*" Porter made a hard swallow and responded, "*Aye, Sir, short and sweet, got it! Sir.*"

"*First Officer, we have a briefing to attend, let's get a move on, Pilot, you have the bridge.*" All eyes on the bridge were still on him as he walked toward the lift. As Nottap and Crawford entered the lift, Crawford turned toward the bridge crew, he gave a thumbs up. The tension in the air was gone, the bridge crew smiled and signaled a thumbs up to each other.

As the lift doors closed, Logan sat down in Nottaps' command chair and barked, "*Listen up, in teams of two, go to the armory, get a sidearm and a short blaster with double the ration of ammunition, and report back quickly.*" The bridge crew looked at him with a bewildered look.

Logan shook his head and sighed, "*Nav reported we have a Mars Trooper vessel following us. What do you think? Do they want a spot of tea with us? Now go and return quickly, we all need to be armed. Comms, establish a link with Minertha Military Command,*" barked Logan.

Porter looked at Logan with a rather annoyed expression and, in a sarcastic voice, said, "*Don't let this go to your head, Sir.*" The other bridge crewmen chuckled, and Logan said in his normal voice, "*Right, I guess I got a little excited there.*" Porter replied sarcastically, "A *little*?" the entire bridge crew laughed, hooped, and hollered.

While in the lift, Nottap looked at Crawford, "*It's going to get worse, I can feel it. So, First Officer, I plan on going rogue in this situation. If you want out, speak up now, what say you?*"

Crawford looked at Nottap with a big smile, "*I'm glad your testicles have finally dropped. I'm in, however, do not panic or second-guess yourself. You're still in Command, Sir.*"

"*Aye, First Officer, my plan might be hasty, but our behinds are in the fire now. I will brief the crew on our situation and ask if anyone would like to go with the EF Troopers, and we will arrange that. Those who choose to stay on board with us may be at risk of ending their careers earlier than planned. The way I see it, First Officer, you and I are done.*"

Crawford replied, "*Sir, is that the last resort option?*" "*No, First Officer, we're in a box now with a limited crew as large as this, twenty-five hundred crewmen. I know some don't want any part of this.*"

Do Not Panic

"This, Sir? What do you mean This?" "Aye, This, we need to make plans for our escape." "Oh, okay, Sir, let's have a chat." Crawford reached over and pulled the stop plunger on the lift. He looked at Nottap and asked, *"How far are you planning on going with, This?"* Nottap sighed, *"Let's look at this from the Gov of Nav Corp and the Galactic Council's point of view.*

One: An Impact Projectile that was too large for planet Aden, was launched under our Command, and we didn't inquire with the Scientists, Engineering Fabrication, Projectile Specialists, or Launcher Crew during the planning or build.

Two: Planet Aden was destroyed, with untold lives lost, and an asteroid belt was created, thank good fortune, it is an asteroid belt and not a hazardous asteroid field.

Three: Planet Mars is seriously damaged and possibly crippled, with untold lives lost. Minertha, could be seriously damaged or in grave peril. To me, that adds up to at least one thousand cycles in confinement.

So, the answer to your question is, all the way. Once in detention, we may be transferred to confinement and not come out. That is not how I want to live or die."

Crawford reached over and pushed the start button on the lift, *"You're going to need new pants, those are too tight for those huge testicles of yours."* Crawford looked at Nottap, *"I said, "do ... not ... panic." Well, Sir, you're in panic mode. That may or may not be the point of view of the Gov of Nav Corp and the Galactic Council.*

However, the Aden Representatives signed a contract you helped formulate. In that contract is a failsafe provision, which is in the provision and exclusions section, it states that in the event the planet is uninhabitable, Planetary Developers will transport your populace to another planet to colonize or build your populace a new planet.

So, let's do our job. We will find them another eight-thousand-mile diameter planet to occupy and transport them there. Better yet, arrange for another PDV with a full crew complement to pick them up and transport them, how hard could that be?

Sir, next you send a message to the Gov of Nav Corp, Galactic Council, and GMF Command to inform them we will execute the failsafe provision. Any help from them would be appreciated.

You remind them you're a principal in the contract, as the Agent for Gov of Nav Corp. You, and the entire crew, cannot be removed from PDV-109 while the contract is in force, and we are executing the Failsafe provision. This is a Civil Matter and not a Criminal Matter or a galactic problem. You also notify Mars with this message. "We are aware of the damage our projectile caused and will respond immediately. We will also start on repairs after we assess the planet."

Also, Sir, send a message to Minertha, "Please advise the people of Aden that the failsafe provision is now being executed by us." By doing this, we are no longer in the fire. Do you agree? Nottap glanced at the ceiling, looked at Crawford, and smiled, "*First Officer, why aren't you a Commander? You're excellent with the men, you're organized, and ...* "

He was cut off by Crawford, who said, "*Ok, ok, stop, stop. Now remember, tell the crew we will do our job, failsafe provision, this is not a criminal matter, it is a civil matter, Agents for Gov of Nav Corp, and we cannot be removed from PDV-109. Got it?*"

"Aye, got it! and I want you to stand behind me, to my right, so I can feel your strength and calmness." Crawford sighed and said, "*Sure.*" The lift doors opened, and the two walked to the main auditorium.

Right behind you CQF

After the announcement by Nottap concluded with the urgent order to shut down the engines and report to the main auditorium for a briefing, Abbott swiftly sent a message to Costello, *"JUMP SHIP NOW."*

Abbott and Costello, their hearts pounding, hurried through their departments, urgently calling out, *"JUMP SHIP NOW."* Abbott turned to Launcher Tech Dodson, his voice filled with urgency, *"Take your group to Inventory Control and secure them. Go easy on the Manager, respect his Title. We will wait for you at the space dock. Be quick, the pilots will not depart unless your group is there, they have stressed, "Leave no man behind." "Aye Chief."*

As the two groups exited the launcher section, they separated. A Launcher crewman noticed the other group trotting in a different direction, he called out, *"Chief, where are they going?"* Abbott replied, *"Tie up loose ends. They will join us at the space dock, follow me."*

At the space dock, Abbott noticed a dock door was open, and one of the Olympus Wrath Landing vessels was missing. He had his men load supplies and climb aboard an Olympus Wrath Landing vessel.

As Dodson and his group arrived, they opened the space dock doors for the two Olympus Wrath vessels and climbed aboard. Costello and his group arrived, they loaded supplies and climbed aboard the second Olympus Wrath vessel, and signaled they were ready to launch.

The two vessels departed and headed for Minertha. Cosby pilot and Nash, copilot of the Olympus Wrath landing vessel, which carried the Launcher Crew, noticed the Olympus Wrath Landing vessel, which had cleared the dock a few moments earlier.

It appeared to be going to Minertha. Nash asked Cosby, "*Who is that?*" Cosby replied, "*I don't know, they are going too slow, so let's get out of here.*" Nash turned on the cloaking device and accelerated to the top velocity.

McDonald, the Olympus Wrath landing vessel pilot that carried the Projectile Specialists, radioed Cosby, "*Right behind you, CQF.*" Nash turned on the rearview monitor. The screen showed the landing skids and underbelly of the other Olympus Wrath, and he screamed.

Cosby looked at Nash, looked at the monitor, back at Nash, "*What? you've never flown, close quarter formation before?*" he turned off the monitor and said, "*Look out the front.*"

Tami

On Minertha, a young mother and her daughter stood on a mound. They held hands as they looked up into the night sky. *"There, honey,"* said Mom, pointing into the night sky. *"Our planet was right about there."*

Tami looked at her mom, *"Mom, do we live here now?"* Tami's Mom looked down at her, *"Yes, the people of Minertha are kind, and this is where we live now." "Will we have a house?" "Yes, honey, we will have a new house." "Mom, I must draw a new picture of us in front of our new house."*

"There you two are." called out Tami's dad, Rob, as he walked up the mound. *"Good news, we get land, animals and our new neighbors will help me build a new home,"* Rob announced, his voice filled with excitement.

As Tami and her parents looked up at the stars, Rob's PDT vibrated. He opened the new message, his heart pounding with anticipation. *"Robert, this is to inform you the Neiubo Planetary Developers are executing the Failsafe Provision and will be searching for a new planet for us to colonize, transportation will also be provided by them."*

He looked at his wife and daughter, their faces lit up with joy as they enjoyed the stars. Tami looked up at Rob and asked, *"Is that your work Daddy? Do you have to leave? I wish you would stay with us."* Rob looked at Tami and said, *"Wish granted."*

He put his PDT in his pocket, stood between them and put his arms around them, his heart filled with love and gratitude. As Robert held his wife and daughter, looking at the stars he noticed this was the first time more stars were visible. He shrugged it off with the thought *"Maybe, their ocean is thinner than on Aden, or maybe they have a leak."*

The End

But wait, there's more...

Planetary Developers Series: Mars, the Remodel, Vol Two.

Commander Nottap and First Officer Crawford deal with missing crewmen. Nottap needs a head count of the remaining crew to start assigning cross training. Crawford realizes they must leave tradition to accomplish their goals on Mars. An unexpected find may save the day.

Mars needs immediate repair, but before that can start, Commander Nottap and crew need to be on the same page. EF Troopers have been ordered to board the PDV and take control of the vessel and crew. Tension is at an all time high within the crew. They must decide their loyalties, Nottap or Gov of Nav Corp.

Half of the crew remind the command staff their contract is for a Maiden Voyage only. This *"Little side job"* is no benefit for them, it only benefits command and the Gov of Nav Corp. Whispers of a mutiny swirl below deck.

As the EF Troopers close in, they are faced with a hard choice. Comply and face detainment or refuse the order to *"Stand down"* and risk attack. Nottap and the remaining crew look to First Officer Crawford for the answer.

Acknowledgements

Thank you for buying this book. I am grateful to have you as a Reader. This is book one of the eight book series.

Cover design by Getcovers.com

Thank you, David and Kelly, for your content and contributions.

Thank you again my valued Readers.

ISBN 979-8-9907842-9-1